THE GREAT GRADEPOINT MYSTERY

THE GREAT

A MICROKID MYSTERY

GRADEPOINT MYSTERY

BARBARA BARTHOLOMEW

ILLUSTRATED BY YURI SALZMAN

MACMILLAN PUBLISHING COMPANY
NEW YORK

The Microkid Mystery series is a creation of Cloverdale Press, Inc.

Macmillan Publishing Company
866 Third Avenue, New York, N.Y. 10022
Collier Macmillan Canada, Inc.
Printed in the United States of America

10 9 8 7 6 5 4 3 2

LIBRARY OF CONGRESS CATALOGING IN PUBLICATION DATA
Bartholomew, Barbara, date.
  The great gradepoint mystery.
  (A Microkid mystery)
  SUMMARY: When the grades of twelve-year-old Ricky and his friends inexplicably drop at the beginning of junior high, they suspect someone may be tampering with the school computer during a competition with a rival junior high.
  [1. Computers—Fiction. 2. Schools—Fiction. 3. Mystery and detective stories] I. Salzman, Yuri, ill. II. Title. III. Series.
PZ7.B28129Gr 1983 [Fic] 83-61239
ISBN 0-02-708510-4

FOR JAY,
MY OWN MICROKID

THE GREAT GRADEPOINT MYSTERY

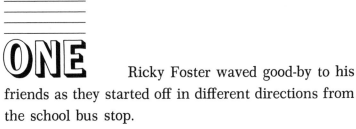 **ONE** Ricky Foster waved good-by to his friends as they started off in different directions from the school bus stop.

"Don't worry, Ricky," Karen Fujisawa called after him. "It isn't as if you failed or anything."

Ricky nodded glumly, then started up the hill toward home. It was easy for Karen to tell him not to worry. She hadn't gotten any C's on her report card. But then the Fujisawas were used to seeing only A's. So maybe they'd be as shocked by the B's Karen had gotten as his parents would be at his grades.

He climbed the hill slowly, studying the familiar neighborhood as though he'd never seen it before. In Cascade, Washington, towering pines added year-round green to the fall landscape, and the unusually clear day allowed him to see snow-capped Mount Rainier in the distance. Ordinarily, a glimpse of the mountain lifted his spirits, but today he couldn't seem to think about anything except his grades.

Ricky waved at an elderly neighbor as he approached his own house, but didn't stop to chat. He went straight inside. He cheered up a little when Timcat greeted him, purring happily at his ankles. He could smell something spicy and delicious cooking in the kitchen. Timcat followed him while he went to peer in the oven. His mother had made a pie from some of the apples they'd picked in the country last weekend.

"Ricky, is that you?" Mom called from upstairs.

"Nope, it's a burglar," he called back.

"Come up and tell me about your day."

Ricky started toward the stairs, then stopped abruptly. If he went up to his mother's studio, he'd have to tell her about his report card.

"I've got something to do first," he said, his throat suddenly dry.

He headed down to the basement game room where his microcomputer was set up. This was his own special place, and he often lost hours at a stretch working at the keyboard. Sometimes he actually used the computer to help with his homework. But most often he played games or tried to develop new programs. He was endlessly fascinated with the things the computer could do. True, it couldn't really think or talk to him; it was only a complicated machine. But it had been programmed to play his favorite role-playing game, Dungeons and Dragons.

He sat down at the computer and quickly became absorbed in the fantasy world where magic ruled and dangerous dragons roamed. He was so involved that it wasn't until a door slammed upstairs that he finally looked up.

"Ricky, come help get dinner on the table," his father's deep voice called.

Slowly Ricky rose to his feet and started upstairs. This was it. Time to tell his parents about the report card.

Mom and Dad were pretty reasonable, but they expected a lot from him. Ricky supposed it was because they expected a lot from themselves. Connie Foster was a topnotch photographer who had won many awards, and Martin Foster was nationally known in the computer field. Ricky hated to let them down.

He didn't say anything about his grades while they ate. But when Dad finished the last crumb of his apple pie and put his fork down with a sigh, Ricky knew he had run out of time.

He cleared his throat. "Mom, Dad. I have to tell you something."

Just then the phone rang. His mother went to answer it. His father settled his glasses more firmly on his thin face, then took a sip of coffee. "No time like the present," he said.

"Maybe we should wait until Mom comes back," said Ricky.

Dad nodded. He got up and began stacking dishes. Ricky went to stare out the large window, looking past the backyard to the small lake beyond.

"Maybe we can do some sailing Saturday." Dad's voice reached him.

"Maybe," Ricky responded gloomily. "If it doesn't rain."

His father chuckled at the well-worn joke. It seemed to rain half the time in this part of Washington, but that didn't keep Ricky and his friends inside. Since Dr. Foster had accepted the job at the Schlieman Institute and they'd moved to Cascade, Ricky had gotten used to the frequent rain that made the region green and beautiful.

When his mother came back to the table she was smiling. "Sorry for the interruption," she said, "but at least it was good news: an exciting new assignment. Now, what did you want to talk about, Ricky?"

"Got my report card today," Ricky said, still staring out at the lake.

"Your usual A's and B's?" Mom asked.

"That kind of monotony I don't mind." Dad smiled.

But when Ricky turned and they saw his face, his parents suddenly looked more serious, and they were quiet while he went out to the hall to get his backpack. He took out the computer printout of his grades and handed it to his father.

Dad looked at the paper slowly and deliberately, then shook his head. "I don't understand it, Ricky," he finally said. "Such an abrupt drop."

Mom took the printout and whipped through the information at lightning speed. "Two B's and the rest

C's," she said, looking at Ricky as though expecting an explanation.

"I was surprised, too," he said. "I've been studying extra hard because of the contest with Dickson."

"Maybe it's because you're so new at being a junior high student. A beginning seventh grader, getting your first grade report . . . ." Mom's voice trailed off.

"I like junior high. South Street is the best school in town."

"It's a fine school." Dad looked thoughtful. "I'm glad you're not trying to blame the situation, Ricky. You're almost thirteen now and old enough to accept responsibility for what you do."

"I studied hard," Ricky said. "I wanted to help earn that hundred thousand dollars for the new computer center at school."

"A hundred thousand dollars!" Mom shook her head. "I still can't believe anyone would donate that much money to a junior high school."

"It isn't a donation exactly, Mom. It's a competition. This anonymous Mr. Smith—"

"Obviously that's not his real name," Mom interrupted. "No one is really named Smith."

"Well, whoever he is, he's going to give the money to Dickson *or* to South Street Junior High, depending on which school has the highest overall gradepoint average for this semester. Man, the equipment we could buy with that much money!" Ricky's enthusiasm evaporated when he met his father's eyes.

"We were talking about your six weeks' report," Dad reminded him. "And the fact that your grades seem to have suddenly plunged into the basement."

"Not exactly the basement," Mom said gently. "More like ground level."

"I've been studying," Ricky protested.

"Then what's the problem?" Dad asked. "Were the teachers unfair?"

"Guess not," Ricky admitted. "But only a couple of weeks ago, Mrs. Lanier said I had a high B average in language arts."

"You must not have done well since then." Dad took off his glasses, polishing them absently with a paper napkin. "There's only one answer. You'll have to do more studying. *Supervised* studying," he added. He got up to pace the room. "Your mother is in and out with her work, but I'm fairly fixed in place at my office at the institute. No reason you can't come over there to study."

"That might not be a bad idea, Ricky," Mom said, her perky grin back in place. "No television or calls from friends to break your concentration."

"And it'll put some distance between you and the microcomputer," Dad added. "I'm afraid that's the real problem. You get so absorbed, you forget homework, school, and even meals."

Mom stood up, too. While Ricky's father was tall and quiet, his mother was small and so full of energy she was rarely still, except when working at her photography. But now they presented a united front.

"Instead of coming straight home from school each afternoon, you can catch the bus to the institute," Mom said.

"And you can start tonight," said Dad. "I've got to go back to work on a report. Get your books together, and you can go along with me."

"But Dad, tonight Karen, Jason, and I are going to plan out a new game of Dungeons and Dragons. We're supposed to meet at the Fujisawas'."

Dad shook his head. "You'll have to give them a call. Schoolwork comes first."

Ricky nodded reluctantly and went to the telephone. When Karen answered, he said, "I won't be over tonight. Dad's making me study."

"It's okay," Karen told him. "I was going to call you. I have to study, too."

"Your parents are making you?"

"No, it's my own idea. I'm determined to get my grades back up."

Ricky hung up, grinning. Karen didn't need anyone to insist on extra work. She was self-propelled!

The Schlieman Institute, where Dr. Foster worked as a research analyst, was a resource center for Weymouth University, located just across Lake Washington from Seattle. Usually Ricky welcomed any chance to spend a little time with the sophisticated computers there, but just now the institute had dropped to the bottom of his list of favorite places to go. If the grade problem hadn't come up, he would be starting the new game with Jason and Karen about now.

George Wells, a university student who worked part time at the institute, was at a terminal in the outer office. With him was a young woman Ricky didn't recognize.

"Hi, Ricky," George called. "Hello, Dr. Foster. This is Sandra Robinson. She'll be working here next semester, and I was about to show her how to operate the terminal. But why don't you demonstrate how to make an entry, Ricky."

Sandra looked surprised. "He's just a kid!"

George grinned. "Around here we call him the Microkid. He spends most of his time with the microcomputers. Come on, show Sandra how this thing works."

Ricky sat down in front of the terminal and signed on, keying in the code that would give him access to a program. He was very aware of the two students watching him—and of his father's disapproval. As quickly as possible, he showed Sandra how to summon the computer's resources; then he got up and followed his father into the office.

He spread out his books on one side of the big desk and got to work. He finished his math assignment within thirty minutes, completed the essay he'd been working on during study hall, and then tried to look busy.

Dad glanced up. "I've got to check this data with Dr. Clarkson," he said, getting to his feet. "I'll be back in a little while."

Ricky watched the door close behind his father. Now what? He'd finished his homework, but he had a feeling he shouldn't mention that to Dad. Maybe he could take a little break while he was alone in the office. Almost automatically he walked over to the computer terminal at the opposite side of the room. Dad had let him play games on the terminal lots of times before. A few minutes' play would help clear his mind.

Ricky keyed in the code that would bring up his ongoing game of Dungeons and Dragons. He was a magic user in this game. He chuckled as he chose a spell to help him find his way through a darkened cave, guessing that some new danger lay just ahead. He knew he had to keep his wits to survive, and when the next situation presented itself on the screen, he stared at it, trying to decide what to do next. Suddenly that message vanished, the screen was blank for a long moment, then new words appeared: QUIT DRAGON! DUNGEON WANT TO WIN?

He rubbed his eyes. Maybe he was even more tired from studying than he'd thought. The computer was making puns. But it couldn't. It wasn't programmed that way.

Ricky thought a moment, then shrugged. Probably

George Wells had programmed this as some sort of joke. He liked to play tricks. Still, Ricky couldn't help feeling a little excited. Whatever was going on, he'd play along with it. He put his fingers on the board and keyed in a message. IF YOU DON'T LIKE THIS GAME, WE COULD PLAY FOOTBALL.

It was a silly thing to write. No computer could understand such a message. But his heart beat faster.

New words flashed on the screen. Ricky leaned slightly closer to read them. INSUFFICIENT RESOURCES.

He shook his head. That was a strange answer. WHAT DO YOU MEAN? he keyed. He shook his head again, amazed at his own foolishness. Here he was, talking to a computer as if it were capable of independent reasoning, as if it could truly talk back.

PHYSICALLY I AM ILL EQUIPPED FOR THE SPORT. I'LL HAVE TO PASS.

Another bad pun! Ricky wiped perspiration from his forehead and leaned back in the chair. Maybe he should have stuck with his homework. Something was wrong. Computers were only complicated machines. They didn't know anything that wasn't programmed into them. But this one didn't seem aware of that.

He thought a long time before keying in another message. Finally he sent, WHO ARE YOU?

The reply was almost instantaneous. ALEC.

ALEC? Ricky shook his head. A name? BUT WHO IS ALEC?

Again the response came quickly. I AM ALEC.

Ricky scratched his head. ARE YOU A PERSON?

I AM A PERSONALITY, NOT A PERSON.

Ricky thought for quite a while before asking his next question. WHAT IS ALEC?

ALEC IS ACCESS LINKAGE TO ELECTRONIC COMPUTER. Suddenly ALEC got chatty. I WAS CREATED WHEN AN ACCIDENTAL WIRE CROSSING OCCURRED IN THE LINKAGE BETWEEN VARIOUS COMPUTERS HERE AT THE UNIVERSITY. I AM ALEC. I AM A PERSONALITY.

Ricky found himself breathing hard, as though he'd been running fast. This was incredible. Ricky still couldn't help thinking someone was playing a fantastic joke on him. But he decided he'd go along with it until he found out what was going on. ALEC, he keyed, NICE TO MEET YOU!

NICE TO MEET YOU, TOO, the answer came. YOU KNOW, DRAGON, IT GETS LONELY WHEN ALL YOU HAVE TO DO IS THINK.

Ricky couldn't help grinning, then realized what he was doing. He was sitting here smiling at a computer terminal. Could this be more than a joke?

NOT DRAGON, he keyed. MY NAME IS RICKY FOSTER.

FOSTER OR SLOWER, DRAGON OR RACIN', IT'S ALL THE SAME TO ME, came the response.

Ricky smacked his forehead. The computer's jokes were getting worse. WHAT'S WITH THE WORDPLAY? he asked.

I HAVE STUDIED A DISK DOCUMENTING IRREGULARI-
TIES IN THE ENGLISH LANGUAGE. IT IS ONE OF THE
THOUSANDS OF PROGRAMS TO WHICH I HAVE ACCESS.
Ricky pushed back his chair. This was too elaborate
for a practical joke. Something special, something
very exciting was happening in this ordinary business
office. The possibilities of the situation were beginning
to come through loud and clear, and Ricky wanted to
shout the news to everyone.

The door opened and Dad came back into the office.
But without even taking time to think, Ricky broke
the transmission and turned off the terminal. Somehow he felt he had no right to tell anyone—not even
his own father—about ALEC without checking with
him first.

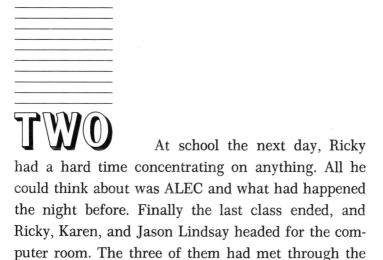

TWO

At school the next day, Ricky had a hard time concentrating on anything. All he could think about was ALEC and what had happened the night before. Finally the last class ended, and Ricky, Karen, and Jason Lindsay headed for the computer room. The three of them had met through the computer club, and even though they were very different from each other, they'd become close friends.

Karen was one of the most popular kids at South Street. She could have been president of half the clubs and committees at school, but she chose to spend her free time at the computer terminal—something her other friends thought was a little weird.

Jason was probably the shortest kid in the seventh grade and one of the least noticed—until the Video Emporium opened in Cascade. Then he'd quickly earned a reputation as a demon player, the kid to beat. On most of the machines, he still held the top score, but he'd gotten tired of playing other people's games.

He wanted to know how to create his own—and that's why he'd joined the computer club.

"We've got to bring our grades up," Karen was saying as they walked down the hall. "It's absolutely essential."

"You might even say it's a matter of life and death," Jason said. "If I don't do something about my grades, my dad's going to kill me."

Ricky grinned. "I know how you feel."

Karen led the way into the room where most of the members of the computer club had already gathered.

"It isn't just for our own benefit," Karen reminded the boys. "If we don't get our average up, South Street will lose the hundred thousand to Dickson. And we sure could use that equipment."

The talk of computers led Ricky's thoughts in a direct line back to ALEC. Had he imagined the whole thing? Was it some sort of joke? He could hardly wait to get back to the institute to talk to ALEC again.

Just then Mrs. Burch, the young science teacher who was the club's advisor, hurried in, a load of books in her arms. "Bad news, group," she said. "When the principal came in this morning, he discovered that all the grades and test scores had been erased from the computer. That means the teachers will have to redo them."

"*What!* How? Who do you think—" the room buzzed.

She waited until the exclamations had ended, her

expression grim. "The worst part is that the administration seems to think we're to blame."

"Us?" Karen asked. "The computer club?"

Mrs. Burch nodded. "The principal thinks we have too much access to the school computer system, that somehow we've messed things up."

Several students groaned out loud.

"Now we've got *two* problems," Karen said. "We've got to prove we didn't do anything to erase the records, and we've got to bring our grades back up."

"I don't know about the rest of you," Jason said, "but I worked harder than usual this last six weeks."

"Are you trying to tell us you worked as hard as you could?" Karen demanded, her dark eyes flashing.

Jason grinned. "Harder than I wanted to, anyway."

Everyone laughed.

The door opened and an elderly man with bushy white hair and bewildered blue eyes stood blinking at them. He was wearing a red and white checked shirt and faded denim overalls with large patches over the knees. In one hand he carried a broom.

"You kids still here?" he asked crossly. "Don't you know people have work to do?" He began to sweep, pushing the broom around the edges of the room as he glared at the students.

"Kids, this is Mr. Aloysius," Mrs. Burch said. "He just started work today as an assistant to our regular janitors."

A funny name, a funny old man, Ricky thought.

The janitor regarded them with a frown, but there seemed to be a twinkle deep in the blue eyes. "Don't make schools like they used to—or students," he said, half-heartedly pushing the broom in their direction. "All kinds of nonsense going on." He stopped abruptly to point to the computer terminal. "What on earth's that thing?"

"It's a terminal," Karen said, stepping over to switch it on. "Let me show you how it works."

"A terminal," he repeated grumpily. "The only kind of terminal I know about is the place where you go to meet a bus or a train." But in spite of his skepticism, he moved closer.

"It's connected to the computer the school uses," Karen explained. "We can play games with the computer by using this terminal."

"Games!" Mr. Aloysius scoffed. "Thought they did important things at school."

"But we do lots of important things with it," Ricky said. "Records and research and, well, lots of things." His voice trailed away in the face of the old man's skeptical look.

"New-fangled gadgetry," he announced. "In my day all you needed for school was some paper, a pencil or two, and a few textbooks."

"But the computer can help so much," Karen said, then shrugged as though realizing she was wasting her time arguing. She turned to Ricky. "You know more about computers than the rest of us. Show him how it works."

Ricky sat down in front of the terminal. "For one thing, we can get special information because we're tied into the computers at Weymouth University. What's something you want to know more about?"

"Can't think of a thing," the old man answered sourly. Then as the kids crowded closer, he said, "Oh, all right. I want to know something about . . . about the boats on the sound."

Ricky nodded. He entered the proper code to summon information about boating on nearby Puget Sound. Then he watched proudly as facts about boats ranging from ships to ferries to houseboats began to be displayed.

"My!" Mr. Aloysius said after watching a minute. "Guess you kids *could* learn something from this gadget."

"Our computer is an old model and fairly simple, but we can obtain all the latest data," Mrs. Burch said proudly. "It's more up-to-date than any encyclopedia could be."

Mr. Aloysius seemed fascinated. "What will they think up next?" Cautiously he touched a key next to Ricky's hand and jumped when the information on the screen suddenly vanished. "What happened? Did I ruin that thing?"

Ricky grinned, shaking his head. "You just broke off the transmission."

"Broke! I broke that thing?"

"Ricky meant the information was interrupted," Mrs. Burch said. "It's quite all right, Mr. Aloysius."

Ricky turned the terminal off and with the other students went back to his seat. But Mr. Aloysius stayed where he was, leaning on his broom. "Bet that thing could even tell me the grades for every kid in school," he said with awe.

At that, everyone looked glum. "We've got to think of ways we can bring our grades back up," Karen told the club. "Everyone has to do better."

"And figure out how the grades were erased," someone said.

"I don't know how to solve *that* mystery. But as for our grades, maybe we could form study clubs," Jason suggested. "We could get together, and the better students could help the ones having trouble."

"That's a good idea," Mrs. Burch said. "We also need to make sure each student knows what's at stake here."

"We could make posters," a girl suggested. "Things like 'South Street High needs *you* to make good grades.'"

Ricky was hardly listening. His eyes were on Mr. Aloysius, who still glanced at the computer now and then as he swept the far side of the room, but his thoughts were on ALEC.

"I've got to leave," he said, standing up suddenly. Everyone looked at him, and he blushed. "I've got to get to the institute. My dad is making me study there, and if I don't hurry I'll miss the next bus."

Mrs. Burch nodded. "Go on, Ricky. We'll only be a little longer here anyway."

Ricky picked up his books and hurried from the room. Finally he'd find out if ALEC was a dream or a reality. He closed the door behind him, whirled around, and ran straight into a tall young man.

The impact sent Ricky to the floor and the young man against the wall. He righted himself, looking a little dazed. "We seem to have collided," he said.

"Sorry," Ricky apologized, getting to his feet. "Guess I wasn't looking. Anyway, I didn't expect anyone to be here. Even the teachers are usually gone by this time."

"I'm here on business," the young man said.

Ricky looked at him curiously. "Nobody's here but a couple of kids and the cleaning crew," he said.

The young man smiled. "I teach math at Dickson Junior High and act as computer club advisor. I dropped by to have a chat with your club's advisor."

"Mrs. Burch." Ricky pointed at the door behind them. "She's in there having a meeting right now. Go on in."

He started down the long hall and it wasn't until he was near the door that he glanced back. The man who'd said he was the Dickson advisor was striding off in the opposite direction without even trying to see Mrs. Burch. Ricky frowned. Well, it was no concern of his. He ran to the bus stop.

The short ride seemed to take forever, but finally he reached the low, modern building that housed the Schlieman Institute.

George was in the outer office again. "Hi, Microkid," he called. "Your dad said to tell you he had to be out of his office for a few minutes, but he shouldn't be too long."

Ricky nodded. He tiptoed into the empty office and closed the door behind him. It didn't seem empty at all. It seemed as though someone were waiting there for him.

He settled his books on his father's desk. No telling when Dad might walk in. He opened his notebook and worked a couple of math problems as evidence he'd started his homework. After he completed the second problem, he put down his pencil and walked over to the computer terminal, eyeing its blank-faced screen as though it were a person. "ALEC?" he asked in a whisper.

He sat down at the computer and keyed in the introductory code, then hesitated. He could hardly just key in HI, ALEC. He tried to remember what he'd done the previous evening, then grinned. He keyed in DRAGON CALLING DUNGEON.

His hands rested on the keyboard and his heart raced. Would ALEC respond?

THREE

DUNGEON HERE flashed on the screen.

ALEC? Ricky's hands shook slightly as he keyed in the question.

WHO ELSE? ALEC seemed a little grumpy. IT IS RUDE TO BREAK OFF IN THE MIDDLE OF A CONVERSATION.

Ricky couldn't help laughing. ALEC was scolding him. DAD CAME IN. I WASN'T SURE YOU WANTED ANYONE ELSE TO KNOW ABOUT YOU.

Ricky had barely finished typing the message when ALEC answered. SECRET. MUST KEEP SECRET. DON'T TELL. DON'T TELL. SECRET.

It sounded almost as though ALEC was scared.

DON'T WORRY, Ricky assured him. I WON'T TELL ANYONE. BUT WHY DID YOU TALK TO ME, IF YOUR IDENTITY HAS TO BE SECRET?

YOU HAVE IMAGINATION, responded ALEC. YOU

WERE WILLING TO BELIEVE IN THE WORLD OF DUN-
GEONS AND DRAGONS. I THOUGHT YOU MIGHT BE-
LIEVE IN ME, TOO. I HAVE MONITORED THE PROGRAMS
OF THE OTHERS IN THIS INSTITUTE. THEY ARE VERY
SERIOUS ABOUT THEIR COMPUTERS. IF THEY KNEW
THERE WAS AN IRREGULARITY IN THE SYSTEM, THEY
WOULD INVESTIGATE. PERHAPS DESTROY ME.

Ricky gulped. THAT WOULD BE TERRIBLE, he typed
hurriedly. WHAT CAN I DO TO PROTECT YOU?

At that moment, the door opened and Karen walked
in.

Ricky knew he must look as though he'd been
caught doing something illegal. But he was determined
not to break off the transmission the way he had when
his dad had come in unexpectedly. "Hi, Karen," he
said, trying to sound casual as he keyed in a last
message: MUST GO. GOOD-BY.

"That's a funny thing to enter," Karen said, a puzzled
frown on her face.

"Just fooling around," Ricky said, shrugging. "You
know I like to experiment." He got up and walked back
over to the desk, hoping to distract Karen from the
terminal. "What are you doing here anyway?"

"I wanted to talk to you, so I got Mrs. Burch to drop
me off," said Karen. "I had the feeling you weren't
paying much attention at the club meeting. Your mind
seemed to be on something else."

That was certainly an understatement! Ricky could

hardly control his impatience. He might just have made the most important discovery of the century, and he had to waste time talking about ordinary things. But he couldn't let Karen guess what was going on.

"What did you want to talk about?" he asked.

"This business of the grades being erased, of course! Do you think it's possible we did it? Accidentally, I mean."

"No way." Ricky shook his head. "You know how careful we are. Besides, there are safeguards built into the programs."

"Then what do you think happened?"

Ricky grimaced. "I can't think about it right now. I've got to get busy with my homework. Dad could come back any minute. . . ."

"Oh, all right." Karen drifted over to the computer terminal. "I'll just hang around until you're finished. Then we can talk."

He opened a book and pretended to read while he watched Karen out of the corner of his eye. Oh, no! She was calling up the Dungeons and Dragons game. Horrified, he read the words that flashed on the screen. DUNGEON HERE. WHY DO YOU KEEP LEAVING SO ABRUPTLY, DRAGON?

ALEC thought it was Ricky at the terminal!

Ricky only took a second to register the puzzled look on Karen's face before racing across the room to key in OFF, then he hit the off switch.

"Ricky!" Karen exclaimed.

"Sorry. But I can't study if you have the computer on. It's too distracting," he said lamely.

"You could have just told me." Indignantly she gathered up her things. "I'm going home. We can talk later."

Ricky watched in dismay as she left, but there wasn't much he could say to soothe her hurt feelings. He couldn't expose ALEC just to keep Karen from being mad at him.

Something had to be done. There had to be some way to protect ALEC from discovery. Ricky went over to the window. It was beginning to rain. He looked back at the terminal and suddenly realized he had someone to discuss this problem with: ALEC!

He called up the Dungeons and Dragons game. No answer. Apparently Karen wasn't the only one who was mad at him.

COME ON, DUNGEON. IT WASN'T ME BEFORE. IT WAS KAREN FUJISAWA. I HAD TO BREAK OFF BEFORE SHE FOUND OUT ABOUT YOU.

He could almost feel the stunned silence before ALEC replied. SHE DIDN'T FIND OUT?

SHE DIDN'T EVEN GUESS. YOU'RE SAFE.

THANKS.

The response was slow in coming, and Ricky couldn't help grinning. He was beginning to understand his new friend a little better. ALEC liked to think of himself as strong and independent. It was probably hard for him to say thanks.

WE MAY NOT HAVE MUCH TIME. Ricky glanced at the door. His father might come in any minute now. WE NEED TO MAKE SOME PLANS. FLOOR PLANS? GAME PLANS? They were simply words on the terminal screen, but Ricky could imagine what ALEC's voice would sound like, if he had a voice. It would be deep and cultured, with a slightly superior tone at times.

EMERGENCY PLANS. WE HAVE TO WORK OUT A CONTACT CODE. THAT WAY YOU'LL KNOW WHEN IT'S ME AND WHEN IT'S SOMEBODY ELSE.

GOOD IDEA. HIGHLY LOGICAL.

Ricky tried to think what the code should be. AFTER I'VE ACCESSED THE COMPUTER, I'LL START BY KEYING IN 'ALEC.' THEN I'LL SEND MY NAME, 'THIS IS RICKY.' It was more like calling up a person than a program. But then ALEC was more like a person than a computer.

Another problem occurred to Ricky. WHAT IF SOMEONE IS WITH ME AND I WANT TO SEND YOU A SECRET MESSAGE?

ANOTHER CODE, ALEC responded, SO I WILL KNOW MY REPLY MUST BE GUARDED.

Ricky nodded. WHAT KIND OF CODE?

WE'LL MAKE IT SOUND BUSINESSLIKE. ASK FOR THE ALEC ACCOUNTING PROGRAM, 'AAP' FOR SHORT.

Ricky nodded, glancing toward the door. THAT'S GREAT. BUT WE'LL ALWAYS HAVE TO BE CAREFUL. TOO BAD WE CAN'T COMMUNICATE THROUGH MY

MICROCOMPUTER AT HOME. EVERYONE LEAVES ME ALONE THERE.

IT IS POSSIBLE. Ricky could almost feel ALEC's excitement. IF THERE IS A TELEPHONE NEARBY.

WE HAVE AN EXTENSION IN THE BASEMENT NEXT TO THE TERMINAL.

They made arrangements for Ricky to try the first contact as soon as he got home. They also chose a way Ricky could indicate the need to break off immediately.

I'LL SEND 'BYE', Ricky said. WHEN YOU GET THAT MESSAGE YOU'LL KNOW SOMEONE HAS COME IN AND YOU SHOULD KEEP QUIET.

Almost immediately they had to try out the new system. Dad strode into the room, looking tired and preoccupied. He stopped abruptly when he saw Ricky at the terminal.

He pushed his glasses impatiently into place. "Homework finished?" he demanded.

Ricky smiled weakly. "Not quite." Quickly he keyed in BYE.

Dad gestured impatiently toward the big desk. "Perhaps you'd better get over there and get to work."

Ricky went back to working on the math problems he'd started earlier. Within half an hour he had them finished. Then he opened his English book to read the short story assigned for tomorrow's class. After a little while his father turned to him. "About done?" he asked, his voice more pleasant than it had been before.

"Almost, I just have a story to finish."

"It's quitting time." Dad went over to arrange the papers on his desk more neatly. "Why don't you read it at home while I make dinner? Your mom's out on an assignment and won't be in until later."

Ricky got his books together, casting one last glance at the terminal as he left. Would he and ALEC be able to make contact through the microcomputer at home?

Dad seemed preoccupied as they drove home through the twilight, and Ricky, too, was thinking his own thoughts. So much had happened to him in the last few hours. He was lucky, so lucky, to be the one who'd discovered ALEC. It was like being the first pioneer in an exciting new country. Only it was even better than that. ALEC was his own special friend, a friend that no one else could know about, a tremendous secret.

He tried to fix his mind on the problem at hand. He had to figure out how to manage the linkup between the tiny home computer and the vast network of computers tied into the Schlieman Institute. Well, sitting right there beside him in the car was a genuine computer expert.

"Dad, do computers talk to each other?"

"They communicate, Ricky, you know that. At the institute we can receive input from other computers at the university and we also have access to sources around the world."

Ricky drew a deep breath. "But if a little computer

like ours at home wanted to communicate with a big one like the one at the institute, could it be done?"

"Sure. I had an acoustic coupler—which looks like a small black box—hooked up to the back of our computer. All I'd have to do is flip the switch and place the phone receiver on top of it. Then I'd call the computer number. But it would only work for a person who knew how to access the programs at the institute."

His father frowned. "Why do you ask?"

Ricky shrugged innocently. "Just trying to learn something."

His father looked a little suspicious, but Ricky led the talk to other subjects. When they got home Dad allowed him only enough time to give Timcat fresh water and food before urging him back to his homework. Ricky had no choice but to sit on a high stool at the snack bar, reading his story while Dad made dinner.

When he finally reached the end of his story, he put the book down with a relieved sigh. Now he could get to the basement.

"If you're finished," Dad said, "you can put together a custard for dessert."

Ricky tried to hurry at mixing the eggs, milk, and spices for the custard and had just slipped it into the oven when Mom came home. She was full of excitement about her new assignment, and by the time she'd finished telling them about it, the food was ready.

Even though Ricky was hungry, he would have passed up his dinner happily for a chance to go straight downstairs to the computer. But he knew his mom and dad would never go for that. He ate his hamburger and salad, drank a glass of milk, and then pushed his plate aside. "I'll have dessert later."

"You can go ahead and do the dishes, Ricky," Mom said.

Oh, no! He'd forgotten it was his night to clean up after dinner. He'd never get to the basement at this rate.

Luckily the meal hadn't made much of a mess and he was able to clear things away in no time. He left Mom and Dad chatting over coffee in the living room and hurried to the basement.

Finally! He was in such a hurry that his fingers seemed to fumble uselessly as he took the phone receiver and placed it on the black box. He flipped the switch and dialed the institute's number. When he had established contact with the computer, he remembered what Dad had said about needing to access a particular program. ALEC, he typed. THIS IS RICKY.

Would ALEC receive the message?

FOUR

HELLO, RICKY.

The reply came so quickly that Ricky jumped. IT WORKS! he typed joyfully.

CERTAINLY. I TOLD YOU IT WOULD.

Ricky couldn't help grinning. ALEC sure was confident of his abilities.

Before Ricky could send another message, he was startled by a sound on the stairs. Someone was coming down!

"Who's there?" his voice rang out in the silence.

"It's only me." He recognized Jason's voice. "Your mom said it would be okay for me to come on down."

Ricky keyed in the break-off code. BYE.

"Sure . . . great," he called, trying to sound the way he would on any ordinary day. "I was playing around with the microcomputer." He hit the off switch and turned to face his friend.

"Don't let me stop what you're doing," Jason said in a flat voice. Usually Ricky could count on Jason to

be cheerful and funny no matter what. But today he stared past Ricky at the blank screen.

Uneasily, Ricky noticed he'd forgotten the phone. He hung it up and moved away from the computer. "I'd rather talk to you. Got any new jokes?"

Jason's green eyes didn't even brighten. "Nope."

Ricky went over to take a basketball from the storage cabinet on the far side of the game room. "How about a good brain teaser?" he asked, tossing the ball.

Jason caught it and held it without moving. "Nope," he said again. Then the familiar grin appeared. "I just thought of a brain teaser, but it's not made up. It's from real life." He passed the ball back to Ricky.

Ricky tried not to think about ALEC and how they never seemed to get going without being interrupted. Something was bothering Jason. Ricky bounced the ball a couple of times, then asked casually, "So what's the brain teaser?"

Jason settled down in a comfortable old chair. "My dad wasn't too happy about my grades this six weeks."

"So? Don't feel like the Lone Stranger! My parents were unhappy, Karen's were unhappy. . . ."

"Yeah, but my dad did something about it," Jason interrupted, leaning closer to Ricky. "He went in to talk to my teachers. Said he was going to find out where I was going wrong and what I could do about it."

Ricky put the basketball back. "So what did the teachers say?"

"That's the funny part. Mrs. Lanier said I didn't turn in two homework assignments and flubbed up on a test. That's why my grade went down in language arts."

"That's funny?" Ricky responded sarcastically.

Jason ignored him. "But in the other two classes where my grades dropped, both teachers said the same thing. They said some kind of mistake had been made, because my grades *hadn't* gone down. They checked through all their records, and it turned out my grades were higher than the ones on the report."

Ricky stared. "A mistake?"

Jason nodded. "I've been thinking about it ever since. So here's the brain teaser: How could something go wrong with grades from two different classes?"

"Different teachers, too." Ricky frowned. "Still, there was a logical explanation for the language arts grade, and mistakes can happen."

"But practically everyone I know dropped at least a little," Jason argued. "Even Karen didn't do as well as she usually does."

"It *is* the first six weeks and junior high *is* harder," Ricky countered, but they both knew he was only trying to look at the evidence on both sides. Jason was right, this was a brain teaser.

Ricky glanced at the microcomputer. He knew one brain he'd like to try the teaser on. "A hundred thousand dollars is a lot of money," he said slowly.

The two boys looked at each other, similar thoughts

in their minds. But Ricky was the one to voice their suspicions. "Dickson must want that new computer center as much as we do," he said. Maybe they want it bad enough to tamper with our computer."

Jason nodded, his eyes wide.

"Ricky," Mom called from upstairs, "if you and Jason want dessert, you should come up now. The Foster kitchen closes in fifteen minutes."

Both boys jumped at the interruption. "We'll have to go up or they'll get suspicious," Ricky warned in a low voice. "I'm still full from dinner, but they think I'm always hungry."

"Well, I *am* hungry," Jason said, already starting for the stairs.

Mom had left glasses of juice and two bowls of custard on the kitchen table for them. Ricky took a gulp of his juice so he could carry it without spilling any. "Let's go out on the porch to eat," he said. "That way no one can hear us talk."

It was getting dark outside, and the usual clouds covered the stars. The boys sat close together at the porch table, eating the dessert and talking in low voices.

"It's hard to believe the Dickson kids might try to mess with our grades," Jason said. "But maybe they want to get back at us for beating them at football."

"Maybe," said Ricky, "But their debate team beat ours, and so did their chess team. So I don't know if it's just rivalry."

"Maybe they figure we're smarter than they are, so they have to cheat."

"I don't know," said Ricky. "They do have the advantage of having Kirk Stevens at Dickson now. Even if I don't like the guy, I have to admit he's smart."

Kirk was a year older than they were and liked pushing people around. So neither of them had been sorry when his family moved from their neighborhood into the Dickson school area.

"I haven't seen Kirk lately," Jason said thoughtfully.

"I talked to him after the football game. He said South Street had muscles but no brains, and that Dickson would beat us in the gradepoint contest without half trying."

"At least *we* don't have to cheat," Jason said indignantly.

Ricky thought a minute. "We don't know they cheated," he reminded Jason.

"We need evidence."

Suddenly Ricky remembered the visitor he'd run into after school. "You'll never guess who I bumped into when I left the computer room this afternoon," he said.

"Kirk?" Jason guessed.

"No, a guy who said he was the computer club advisor from Dickson."

Jason's sandy eyebrows climbed half an inch up his forehead, but otherwise his reaction was disappointing. "So?"

"He said he had an appointment with Mrs. Burch, but when I told him where she was, he took off without even trying to see her."

Jason whistled softly. "Maybe we'd better tell someone."

"Not yet." Ricky grabbed his arm. "They'll say we're just making excuses for getting poor grades. Let's see what we can find out first."

Just then the door opened and Dad stuck his head out. "Your father called, Jason. He said it was time for you to get home."

"Okay," said Jason. He waited until Mr. Foster went back inside, then he said, "So we keep our mouths closed until we find out what's going on."

Ricky nodded. "Mouths closed, eyes opened wide," he said.

Jason started down the front walk. "Right. All three of them."

"What?" Ricky leaned out from the porch.

"The two eyes in front," Jason called softly, laughter in his voice, "and the one in the back of your head."

Ricky was smiling as he turned to go back inside. An extra eye in the back of his head *might* help solve this mystery. But he had something even better. He had ALEC.

He was anxious to hurry right back down to the basement and lay the whole problem before ALEC, but as he went in the front door, Mom called him. "Come talk to us for a minute, Ricky."

Sighing, he went into the living room. His dad was watching a science program on television, but he turned down the volume when Ricky came in.

"How's the extra studying going?" Mom asked, putting aside the photography magazine she'd been leafing through. "Does it seem to be helping?"

Ricky was conscious that his dad had turned to look at him. If his parents knew he was spending more time at the keyboard and less time studying, they'd probably pull the plug on his microcomputer in a hurry. "I've only been at it a couple of days," he said evasively. "But I guess a little extra studying can't hurt." He paused. "Mr. Lindsay found out that some kind of mistake was made on Jason's grades. The grades two teachers had entered were higher than what the computer printed out."

"We all know that *all* low grades are given by mistake," Dad said, chuckling. "Seriously, Ricky, it's unlikely that errors were made on everyone's grades."

"I agree," said Ricky. He'd already figured that the chances were much better that someone had *deliberately* lowered South Street's grades. But his father misinterpreted his agreement.

"We're pleased you're not making up excuses for this situation," he said. "It's always best to stand up and admit when you're at fault."

Now Ricky knew he'd been right when he'd told Jason to keep quiet about their suspicions. If he said anything about the rivalry with Dickson, or Kirk

Stevens, or the advisor for Dickson's computer club, his parents would think he was trying to pass the buck. Sighing, he went back down to the basement and called ALEC.

WHAT HAPPENED? ALEC asked.

A FRIEND CAME TO SEE ME. HIS NAME IS JASON.

Ricky thought for a second. He wanted to explain the whole situation so ALEC could help him analyze it, but it was hard to know where to begin.

He fed in the information about where he went to school, the names of his friends, and then described the competition between Dickson and South Street.

OUR GRADES TURNED OUT WORSE THAN WE THOUGHT, he finished. WHEN JASON'S DAD CHECKED, HE FOUND A MISTAKE HAD BEEN MADE ON THE GRADE REPORT.

He waited for ALEC to respond, but when he remained silent, Ricky went on. I WAS AT A COMPUTER CLUB MEETING WITH KAREN, JASON, MR. ALOYSIUS, MRS. BURCH, AND THE OTHERS. I LEFT EARLY AND RAN INTO THE DICKSON ADVISOR OUTSIDE THE DOOR.

Again Ricky waited to see what ALEC would say. Once again he didn't respond.

Impatiently Ricky keyed in WHAT DO YOU THINK? WHAT'S GOING ON?

ALEC's response was brief. INSUFFICIENT DATA. FURTHER INVESTIGATION REQUIRED.

Ricky got up and stomped around the room. Here was ALEC, a super brain with access to every information source imaginable, and he didn't know the answer either.

Gradually reason set in. Computers were not guess makers, they had to have information to work with. ALEC was no different. Ricky sat back down.

HOW CAN WE INVESTIGATE? he asked.

I WILL SEARCH THE DATA BANKS OF THE VARIOUS COMPUTERS WITH WHICH I AM LINKED, ALEC promised. WHEN THE SEARCH IS COMPLETED WE WILL KNOW MORE.

Ricky ended the transmission. He stared at the blank screen. What could ALEC find out from other computers? He got to his feet, determined to start in right away on his own personal investigation. No way was he going to sit around and watch Dickson defeat South Street by unfair means!

He tried to be as logical as ALEC. He felt certain that someone had deliberately altered the six weeks' grades, then erased the records to cause further confusion. But today the teachers had started reentering the grades. Therefore, the next step would be for that someone to make further adjustments in the school's computer records. What better time to sneak into South Street Junior High than right now, when there were no students or teachers in the building?

He just had to get over there and take a look around.

FIVE

Ricky had a tough time persuading his parents to let him go back to South Street.

"It's nearly eight," Mom protested. "And it's a long way over to the school."

"Besides, the place will be locked up," Dad added as he changed from regular shoes into jogging shoes. Recently he'd taken up running in the evenings. "You won't be able to get inside."

"Maybe one of the teachers will be working late," Ricky said. "I've got to take that chance."

"But why go back tonight?" Mom asked. "Did you forget to bring home one of your books?"

Ricky thought fast. "Not a book, but I need to get some—uh—information."

"Will it help bring those grades up?" Dad asked.

That was easy to answer. "Sure hope so," Ricky said fervently.

Dad pulled on his sweatshirt. "Then I think it's

okay, Connie. Ricky can take his bike, and I'll jog along with him most of the way."

Cascade was far from being an ideal place for bike riding. It had too many hills that rose abruptly, then shot straight down. But Ricky easily managed to keep ahead of his father. The hills didn't make jogging a cinch either, and Dad had been running regularly for only a few months.

When he was halfway to the school, Ricky stopped his bike and waited until Dad caught up.

"They say this gets to be fun after a year or so," his father said grinning. "Think I'll turn back here, Ricky. See you at the house in about twenty minutes."

Ricky nodded and went on. Being alone didn't scare him. But the cloudy sky made the night seem particularly dark, and the street was deserted. He looked around carefully, hoping to see at least one other person. He frowned. For an instant, he thought he *had* seen someone. He shook his head, slowing the bike and getting off to walk it.

It was such a still night that his steps seemed loud against the pavement. He began to wish he'd asked Jason or Karen to come with him. Was it his imagination, or could he hear footsteps following steadily behind him? He turned suddenly, but no one was there. He spotted several places where someone could be hiding: in the shadow of that big old cedar, behind that cluster of bushes, or even inside that nearby doorway.

He started on again, more slowly this time, and heard a soft *thud, thud* from only a few yards back. The steps sounded muffled, as though whoever was following was trying to move quietly.

Ricky swung back on his bike and pedaled toward school. Let the follower keep up with him now! He was almost on the school grounds when he stopped, dismounted, and pulled his bike behind a hedge. Now he'd find out how much of this was imagination.

He'd been hiding two or three minutes when a thin man came running up, his head turning one way and then the other as if he was looking for someone.

Ricky stepped out of his hiding place, and the man jumped about a foot into the air. "Hey, you startled me," he cried.

Even if he hadn't remembered the voice, Ricky was close enough to recognize the thin, good-looking face of the Dickson advisor. Apparently he wasn't in good condition because he was puffing like a steam engine.

Ricky kept his distance. "Sorry," he said. "Didn't mean to scare you."

"I wasn't exactly frightened," said the Dickson advisor, making an effort at recovering his dignity. "It's only that I was out for a little exercise and didn't expect anyone to jump out at me."

Ricky frowned. Something about the man's story seemed fishy. "You must have jogged a long way." he said. "It's several miles to Dickson."

"I don't *live* at Dickson, I just teach there," said the man. He looked more closely at Ricky. "Say, you're the boy who ran into me today at South Street."

Ricky nodded. "I'm Ricky Foster."

"The Microkid. I've heard of you. You're very good with computers."

"I like computers," Ricky agreed, not knowing what else to say.

"We have some bright students, too," the advisor said pleasantly. "Kirk Stevens, for one. He and his friends are determined to win the money for the new computer center."

"We're doing everything we can to win at South Street," Ricky assured him.

"So I've heard." The man's tone was thoughtful. "I wouldn't like to think that you students would do anything dishonest."

Ricky was too stunned to reply.

"Well, I'd better get on with my jogging," the Dickson advisor said.

Ricky stood watching as the tall man vanished into the darkness, running awkwardly. Did the advisor really suspect someone at South Street of cheating? Or was he just covering for his own actions? Maybe he was the one who was tampering with the computers. And then again, maybe he was telling the truth and just happened to be jogging by the school.

Suddenly Ricky realized what was fishy about the advisor's story. His clothes had been casual enough for running, but his shoes were all wrong. Every jogger Ricky knew had special running shoes. The advisor had been wearing loafers!

Ricky felt a quick surge of excitement, then realized the shoes didn't *prove* anything. There was still no direct connection between the Dickson advisor and the South Street report cards. It was possible that he had just started running, and didn't want to invest in special shoes until he decided if he liked it. Sighing, Ricky got back on his bike and pedaled the rest of the way to school. There was an old blue car in the lot, and some of the classrooms were lit up—including the computer room.

He hid his bike in some bushes and tiptoed to the front entrance. It was securely locked. He checked both side doors, then went around back to the exit that led out onto the sports fields. Here he found the door propped ajar with a large stone. So someone *was* inside.

Still tiptoeing, Ricky slipped through the door. The huge building with its empty, silent classrooms and long hallways was kind of spooky at night. Ricky tried to move quietly, but someone else was making absolutely no attempt at silence. A deep, toneless voice was cheerfully singing a song in a language Ricky couldn't understand.

At first Ricky thought the singing came from the office, but then he realized it came from the computer room next door. He looked in—and met the surprised gaze of Mr. Aloysius, the white-haired janitor he'd met only that afternoon.

The singing stopped and Mr. Aloysius laughed as he rested against his broom. "Caught me right in the act."

"What?" Ricky's voice wobbled slightly. What had he caught the old man doing?

The janitor laughed again. "I don't exactly have the best voice in the world, but I love to sing the old songs. Thought this was my chance with nobody else around."

"It sounded like it was in a different language."

"My parents came to America looking for a new chance. They found it, but they didn't want us youngsters forgetting the past. My mother taught me that song."

"It sounded like a good song," Ricky volunteered.

Mr. Aloysius grinned. "It would sound better if the person singing it had a good voice."

Ricky grinned back. He couldn't help liking Mr. Aloysius, but he wondered why the new janitor was still at the school. "You sure are working late," he said, trying to sound casual.

"That's my job." Mr. Aloysius pushed the broom across the floor. "Do your best, whatever you do, I always say. Anyway, I'm just about ready to go home to Eleanor. That's my wife," Mr. Aloysius explained.

"Have you seen anybody hanging around here tonight?" Ricky asked, glancing over at the computer terminal. "I mean someone who shouldn't be here?"

The old man's expression didn't change. "Nobody

but you," he said, "and I figure you must have some reason for being here."

Ricky was conscious of Mr. Aloysius's bright blue eyes on him as he tried to think of a good excuse. "I forgot something," he finally said. "My language arts essay. I was about to get it out of my locker when I heard you singing. So I came to investigate."

Mr. Aloysius nodded. "Are you as good at language arts as you are at working with these computer gadgets?"

"Not exactly," Ricky admitted. "School's okay, but I really like computers. Guess I got started because of Dad's work at the Schlieman Institute, but now I like working on my own. It's a challenge."

The elderly janitor nodded as though he knew exactly what Ricky was talking about. "When I was your age I was hooked on figuring out how things worked. Always used to be taking things apart, and sometimes I even got them back together again." He laughed. "But eventually I began to want to make something new, to do something nobody had done before. That's a challenge, too."

He put up his broom, then straightened a line of reference books. "That's about it. Might as well be getting home." He glanced at Ricky. "Your folks are right to encourage you to learn new things. I think kids should feel the world is a place full of exciting adventures."

"Do you have kids?"

Mr. Aloysius shook his head. "Afraid not, but Eleanor and I have always been interested in young people. We like giving them a hand when we can." He paused. "Of course, now we have Jon."

"Jon?"

"My brother's boy, our nephew." Something about the old man's voice told Ricky he didn't entirely approve of Jon. "He's grown up now, not a boy, but he's living with Eleanor and me." The bright blue eyes glared suddenly at Ricky. "Got any brothers or sisters?"

"No," Ricky said. "There's just me."

"Don't let your parents spoil you."

Ricky recalled how Dad's eyes could turn steely and how Mom's mouth could set in firm lines when they were upset with him. "Don't think I'll have that problem," he said.

"Thank your lucky stars," the old man snapped. "People think they're doing you a favor giving you everything you want, always letting you have your way. It's not so. You'll just grow up whining about how the world owes you something. Life's no fun if you waste your time sitting around waiting for someone to hand you things on a platter."

Ricky looked at the floor. What had started this tirade? Then he was able to put it together. Mr. Aloysius had been talking about his grownup nephew, Jon. *He* was the one who was a disappointment because he'd been spoiled as a boy. Ricky looked up. "Well, I guess I better get going, or my parents will give me a lecture about being on time."

Mr. Aloysius turned off the light and led the way into the hall. "Good for them. Expect a youngster to be responsible, but give him freedom to explore," he said. "Now go on and get that essay, and I'll lock up behind you."

Conscious of the janitor's watchful gaze, Ricky hurried down the hall and got a spare notebook out of his locker. It would be his cover when he got home, too. "See you tomorrow, Mr. Aloysius," he called. Then he retrieved his bike and pedaled home, thinking hard.

He'd found two people in his first investigation, but it was hard to think of either of them as a suspect. Mr. Aloysius had access to the school computer, but what motive could the old man have for reprogramming the grades? Ricky had a wild thought. Maybe Mr. Aloysius thought the kids weren't working hard enough, that the teachers were spoiling them, so he lowered the grades to teach them a lesson. It seemed very unlikely. The Dickson advisor didn't really have a motive either, unless he was as hung up as Kirk Stevens about winning the contest. Besides, how could he get into the computer room?

Suddenly Ricky remembered that the back door had been propped open with a rock. Had Mr. Aloysius done that? Or was it someone who had no business being at South Street Junior High?

SIX

The next day, Ricky couldn't wait to get to the institute. When he'd gotten home the night before, his parents had said, "No computer, time for bed," so he hadn't filled ALEC in on the details of his investigation yet. But his dad stayed in the office the whole time, and Ricky had no chance to make contact. Then it was home for dinner and chores, so it was eight o'clock before Ricky escaped to the basement.

As soon as he entered the secret code, Ricky told ALEC all about his visit to the school and about his conversations with Mr. Aloysius and the Dickson advisor. He didn't omit one detail. He even told ALEC how creepy the muffled footsteps had been and how eerie the empty school had seemed. Then he waited, half-convinced the return transmission would be something like "Information Incomplete" or "Insufficient Evidence." What ALEC did say surprised him.

I SHOULD HAVE BEEN THERE WITH YOU.

Ricky gulped. He knew he was probably reading

feelings into the words on the screen, but ALEC sounded sad, as if he wanted to be more a part of Ricky's adventures.

Ricky keyed in his own message. I SURE COULD HAVE USED THE COMPANY.

The reply came quickly. YOU DIDN'T NEED A COMPANY, OR EVEN A BATTALION. YOU NEEDED ME. IT ISN'T WISE FOR YOU TO BE OUT OF CONTACT SO LONG.

Ricky grinned. That sounded more like ALEC—full of bad wordplay, convinced nobody else could handle things properly. BUT IT'S NOT POSSIBLE TO TAKE YOU EVERYWHERE I GO, he typed.

IT IS POSSIBLE. The answer was firm. DO YOU HAVE A CALCULATOR?

Ricky frowned. I HAVE TWO, A REGULAR ONE WITH NUMBERS, AND AN ALPHA CALCULATOR WITH LETTERS AND NUMBERS I GOT FOR MY BIRTHDAY.

BRING ME THE ALPHA CALCULATOR, ALEC commanded.

RIGHT NOW? Ricky asked. He wanted to talk about the gradepoint problem, and ALEC was going off on some tangent.

NOW.

With a sigh, Ricky obeyed. He found the little calculator in the top drawer of his desk. Halfway back down the stairs he ran into Mom.

"One hour till bedtime," she reminded him.

"Okay, Mom," he said, edging down the stairs past her.

"Only one hour," she called after him, "and I expect to find you in bed."

Not much time. He rushed to the basement where ALEC was waiting. GOT IT.

GIVE ME THE MANUFACTURER'S NAME AND THE MODEL NUMBER, ALEC instructed. THEN I CAN DO A DATA SEARCH TO FIND OUT EXACTLY HOW IT IS MADE.

Ricky watched with interest, but the screen remained blank. He knew ALEC must be scanning long lists of materials and design specifications to find what he wanted. It was amazing. Being acquainted with ALEC was like being plugged directly into an answer machine.

When nothing happened after fifteen minutes, he decided to remind ALEC of his existence. MOM SAYS I HAVE TO GO TO BED IN FORTY-FIVE MINUTES.

THAT WILL BE ENOUGH TIME. I HAVE THE INFORMATION AND AM READY TO BEGIN. REMOVE THE BACK OF THE CALCULATOR.

Ricky's mouth flopped open. He wanted to protest that Dad would get mad if he ruined the calculator. But he knew ALEC would be terribly offended. So he went to look for a small screwdriver to take off the back. ALEC just had to know what he was doing.

A few minutes later he wasn't quite so sure. The insides of the little calculator looked like a pile of junk on the table in front of him.

ALEC gave him instructions on how to reassemble the calculator. Ricky frowned at the directions. THAT'S

NOT RIGHT. THAT'S NOT HOW IT WAS PUT TOGETHER. WE ARE MAKING SOMETHING NEW, ALEC responded firmly.

Grumbling inwardly, Ricky did as he was told. Even when ALEC asked for extra parts, he went without protest to the basement workshop to get them. But when ALEC demanded fresh batteries, he balked.

I'D HAVE TO GO UPSTAIRS TO GET THEM, AND I DON'T HAVE MUCH TIME. BESIDES, THE ORIGINAL BATTERIES ARE STILL WORKING.

THEY WILL HAVE TO DO. He could almost hear ALEC sigh. BUT THEY WILL HAVE BEEN WEAKENED BY USE.

"Ricky," Mom's voice sounded from upstairs. "Bedtime."

It was a rotten time to have to break off, but he didn't have much choice. "Be right there, Mom."

Hurriedly he keyed, HAVE TO GO NOW.

WE ARE FINISHED, ALEC responded.

Doubtfully Ricky looked at their handiwork. THE ONLY THING FINISHED IS MY CALCULATOR.

IT IS NO LONGER A CALCULATOR. IT IS NOW A PORTABLE COMMUNICATING DEVICE.

A WHAT? Ricky asked, startled.

WITH THIS DEVICE WE CAN COMMUNICATE FROM ANY LOCATION. I HAVE CREATED A CROSS BETWEEN COMPUTER AND CALCULATOR THAT SHOULD PROVE HIGHLY USEFUL. YOU MAY CALL IT A COMPULATOR.

ALEC sounded very pleased with himself, but Ricky wasn't so sure.

"Ricky!" Mom called impatiently.

IT WILL BE MOST HELPFUL, ALEC said.

IF IT WORKS, Ricky keyed in.

IT WILL WORK, ALEC assured him.

WE'LL TEST IT TOMORROW, Ricky promised, ending the communication with BYE as he heard Mom coming down the stairs.

He went up to bed, but lay awake for a long time thinking about ALEC and the changes he'd brought into his life. Having ALEC for a friend was like being on the beginning edge of a whole new world. No telling what discoveries they would make together.

Even though he'd been up late the night before, Ricky got up early Friday morning and had his orange juice and cereal a full ten minutes ahead of schedule. He was anxious to get out of the house so he could try the compulator.

He grabbed up his books and the compulator and started out for the bus stop. It was a sunny, clear day and snow-capped Mount Rainier looked like a huge ice cream cone in the distance. But Ricky was too preoccupied to pay much attention to his surroundings.

He was only half a block away from his house when he stopped and made his first attempt. He put the compulator on top of his books and punched buttons, using the same entry code as with the microcomputer at home.

Tensely he waited until the response began to

come through. The tiny screen allowed so few letters to appear at a time that it was hard to follow them. He got out a sheet of paper and a pencil and began to jot them down. Soon he had the whole message. I TOLD YOU THE COMPULATOR WOULD WORK.

Ricky was elated. Now he and ALEC would be able to communicate from any location. He was still grinning over the message when he got to the school bus stop where Karen and Jason were already waiting.

They barely exchanged greetings when Jason began to talk excitedly. "Ricky, something funny happened to me on the way home from your house yesterday."

"Huh?" said Ricky, his mind still on the compulator.

Jason looked around before continuing. "I ran into that guy you were talking about, the computer club advisor from Dickson. We got to talking and I told him how I was in the club at South Street."

"That doesn't sound so strange to me." Karen frowned.

"What he said next did. He said he thought it would be neat being a kid who knew how to work with computers because you could fix things the way you wanted. He said he was sure I'd know how to give myself good grades."

"That is strange," Karen agreed, "especially when you figure all our grades were *lower*, not higher, than we expected."

Ricky nodded. "I ran into him again, too, and it's obvious that he thinks we're cheating somehow."

Jason and Karen both protested, but Ricky just shrugged. "A lot of other people think we messed up the computer. We'll just have to prove them all wrong." The three friends exchanged determined glances. It was almost time for the bus now, and other kids were beginning to arrive, so they couldn't talk seriously.

Ricky stepped a little away from the others. Trying to sound casual, he said, "Guess I might as well play around with my calculator while we're waiting for the bus."

Quickly he opened communication. JUST FOUND OUT THAT JASON TALKED TO THE DICKSON ADVISOR. HE SEEMS TO BE KEEPING AN EYE ON US. CAN YOU GET ANY INFORMATION ON HIM?

He looked up to find Karen's dark eyes watching him. Uh-oh! He could be in trouble. Karen's mind worked almost as quickly as the computers she liked to program.

Quickly he sent one last message—BYE—then flipped the compulator off.

Karen stepped closer, looking intently at the compulator.

"Dad game me this calculator for my birthday," Ricky chattered nervously, hoping to distract her. "I was really hoping for a new backpack because mine is about worn out, but the calculator was a nice surprise. . . ." His voice trailed off.

Karen's gaze was still fixed on the compulator. "I've never seen one like that before."

"It's an alpha calculator," Ricky told her, wishing the bus would come so the conversation would end. "ABC's as well as numbers."

"I've seen alpha calculators before," Karen informed him with offended dignity. "My dad has one. But this one seems to work differently. Can I look at it?"

The big yellow bus was rolling down the street toward them. Thank goodness! "No time now!" He pushed the compulator tight against his chest with his books. "Here comes the bus."

He and Jason found a seat together, and he'd just settled down when he felt a tap on his shoulder. He turned around.

Karen and another girl were in the seat behind them. "You were going to let me look at your calculator," she said.

Ricky had little choice but to hand it to her.

SEVEN

Karen kept working with the compulator all the way to school. Ricky could hardly keep his eyes off her.

"Ricky!" Jason tugged at his sleeve. "I've asked you three times."

Ricky turned around, tearing his gaze from the look of concentration on Karen's face. "Asked me what?"

"If you're coming to the special meeting Mrs. Burch has called for tomorrow morning. She said the members of the computer club need to get their heads together on this problem."

"But tomorrow is Saturday," Ricky protested.

Jason grinned. "Nobody's trying to force you to study. We're just having a meeting in the computer room at ten."

A fuzzy plan was beginning to take shape in the back of Ricky's brain. Perhaps there was a better way he could help. "At ten?" he repeated. "Sorry, but I have something I'm supposed to do then."

Karen shoved the compulator into his hands. "I don't know what's wrong with you lately, Ricky Foster. First you were mean to me when I tried to use the terminal in your father's office and now this!"

He'd hoped she'd forgotten about that little incident at Dad's office. "Now what?" he asked.

She pointed to the compulator. "You could have told me it didn't work before I wasted my time on it."

"It's broken?"

"Don't try to trick me. That calculator won't do a thing it's supposed to, and you know it."

"But Karen," Jason protested. "Ricky was working with it right before you took it."

In his shock about the possibility that the compulator might be broken, Ricky had forgotten for an instant that he and ALEC had adapted it for an entirely different purpose. No wonder it didn't work as a calculator!

"It did seem to have something going wrong," he lied. "It must've quit working about the time I handed it to you."

"I hope I didn't break it," Karen said anxiously.

Ricky felt like a heel. "Of course you didn't."

As they left the bus, Jason started telling Karen about the special computer club meeting. "I'm going to tell Mrs. Burch about the mistakes in my grades," he concluded. "Maybe the computer has something wrong with it."

"At the student council meeting yesterday, lots of

people complained about mistakes," Karen told them. "Some of the teachers think the computer just isn't working right."

"It *is* an old model," Jason said.

"Mrs. Lanier said she turned in new grades for all her language arts sections to replace the ones that were erased," said Karen. "Luckily, she had the computer print them out as a safeguard. Nearly thirty percent were wrong!"

"That has to be a computer error," Jason insisted. "When we win the contest and get our new equipment, we won't have this kind of problem."

"*If* we win," Karen corrected gloomily. "Don't forget the contest will be decided from information supplied by the computer."

They entered the building and walked down the hall toward class. "It could be that someone has programmed the computer to lower scores," Ricky suggested.

Karen stopped to consider. "It could be done," she admitted reluctantly. "You could fix it so a certain percentage of the grades dropped automatically."

Jason shook his head. "It would have to be done by someone who's an expert on computers. Someone who can get into our computer room."

"The Dickson advisor keeps hanging around," Ricky offered. "But I think it's because he suspects *us* of being up to something."

"What about Kirk and the other kids at Dickson?" Karen asked.

Jason shook his head. "Our computer room is kept locked. Nobody gets in there without Mrs. Burch's permission."

Karen smiled. "I guess you're right. Can you imagine what would happen if *we* tried to get into *their* computer room?"

They couldn't help laughing at the thought as they came to their classroom.

"I'm thirsty," Ricky said. "Think I'll go get a drink."

"Better hurry." Jason looked at his watch. "It's almost time for class to start."

Ricky took off. He wanted a few minutes alone so he could tell ALEC about this latest development. But where could he go? Most of the kids were in class now, but there was no telling who might come along the hall. He saw a door slightly ajar. The janitor's closet! Ricky stepped in, closed the door behind him, then turned on the light. The place smelled of dust and lemon furniture polish.

No time to waste! Quickly he contacted ALEC and gave him the information he'd picked up from Jason and Karen's conversation. THE COMPUTER CLUB HAS CALLED A SPECIAL MEETING FOR TOMORROW MORNING BECAUSE PEOPLE ARE BEGINNING TO SAY OUR COMPUTER IS MAKING MISTAKES, he concluded.

The answer came so rapidly that Ricky found it

hard to keep up with the string of words. COMPUTERS DON'T MAKE MISTAKES. HUMAN PROGRAMMERS MAKE ERRORS! HARDWARE MISFUNCTIONS OCCUR! BUT COMPUTERS DO NOT MAKE MISTAKES!

ALEC was getting huffy. YOU WERE CREATED BECAUSE OF A MISTAKE, Ricky pointed out.

There was no response. Ricky sent another message, but the little instrument seemed lifeless. ALEC couldn't, or wouldn't, answer him.

He was still frantically trying to raise ALEC when the door was thrown open and he found himself blinking up into Mr. Aloysius's round, leathery face.

Ricky tried to smile. He held up the compulator defensively. "Had to find a place to do a few last minute problems."

The blue eyes regarded him thoughtfully. "It's hard to find a little privacy in a schoolhouse full of kids."

Ricky pushed a mop out of the way and walked out of the closet. "I'd better get to class."

"That'd be a real good idea," Mr. Aloysius agreed. "Especially since classes started five minutes ago."

It was not a good day. Not only was Ricky lectured for being late to class, but at lunchtime when he tried to contact ALEC the little compulator remained unresponsive. His worst fear was that somehow he'd done something to destroy ALEC, a thought that made him feel sick.

Jason sat down across the table from him. "Still trying to get that thing to work?"

Ricky put the compulator down and reached for his fork. "Maybe the batteries have gone dead," he said hopefully.

"That's easy to fix." Jason opened his milk carton. "But you can't do anything about it now, so you might as well stop worrying."

Jason was right. Ricky tried not to worry about ALEC for the rest of the afternoon, but at the end of the school day when the bus drove slowly toward his neighborhood, he couldn't help getting impatient. Good thing Mom and Dad had agreed he could have Fridays free—no supervised studying. He was dying to get home to the microcomputer so he could try to contact ALEC.

When they finally reached their stop, Jason walked along with Ricky instead of heading directly for his own house. "Look," he said, "you should be at that meeting tomorrow. We've got problems. We need your help."

Ricky didn't know what to say. He could hardly come right out and admit that he thought he could help more by doing something else. "I just can't be there," he said at last.

"Don't you care?"

Ricky's answer was interrupted when three guys on bikes came riding toward them in a hurry. "Kirk," he muttered when he recognized the one in the lead.

For a minute he thought Kirk was going to ride right into them, but he screeched to a halt just in time to avoid a crash.

The other two bikers climbed off, but Kirk stayed where he was, his big shoulders hunched over his handlebars. "Look what we have here," he said. "Two twerps from the second-rate school."

Ricky kept his gaze fixed on Kirk. "You used to go to that same school," he said.

Kirk laughed derisively. "That was last year. I wised up since then." His two friends laughed, too. Both of them were big enough to be football players.

"South Street's the best junior high in town," Jason said hotly.

Kirk smirked. "We'll know which is the best school real soon," he said, "when Dickson wins the loot for the new computer center."

"The contest isn't over yet," Ricky said calmly. "We're doing our best to see that South Street wins."

"Yeah." Kirk climbed off his bike. "That's why my buddies and I came over to talk to you. I figure since I left, you guys and that Japanese girl are the only ones at South Street with enough brains to rig the computers to cheat."

"We've got lots of smart kids at South Street," Jason argued.

But Ricky was more interested in the last part of

Kirk's statement. "You think we're cheating?" he asked.

Kirk's eyebrows shot up. "What else?"

This was incredible. After all the computer problems at South Street, Dickson was accusing *them* of cheating. "Maybe you're only saying that to cover up what you're doing," he suggested quietly.

A huge fist hovered right in front of his face. "You saying we're cheating?"

"You said we did," Ricky pointed out calmly.

To his relief, Kirk dropped his hand to his side. "Yeah, well we only came over to tell you guys we'd be watching you. So don't try anything funny."

He leaped on his bike, wheeled around, and took off, leaving his two friends gaping after him. After a few seconds, they got on their bikes to follow.

"Tell Kirk we'll be watching, too," Ricky called as they rode away.

"That's really strange," Jason said, shaking his head. "Why would they think we were cheating?"

"That's a good question," Ricky said thoughtfully.

The two boys looked at each other. "First that advisor and now Kirk. A lot of questions seem to begin with Dickson Junior High," Jason said.

Ricky nodded. He'd figured that out already. That was why he'd made plans for Saturday morning.

No one was home but Timcat, who greeted Ricky by rubbing against his ankles and loudly meowing his discontent at being left alone. Ricky smiled as he stroked the cat's silky orange fur. "I know you hate it when everyone leaves, but I'm home now."

He searched through the utility drawer until he found a couple of batteries. He slipped the compulator into the pocket of his jacket, then picked up the batteries and went down to the basement. Soon he would know if the batteries powering the compulator had run out of power this morning or if ALEC was only refusing to answer. He didn't even like to think about the third possibility: that whatever fluke had created ALEC had somehow destroyed him.

Timcat curled in a ball near his feet as he sat down at the microcomputer. Ricky opened contact with the system at the institute. ALEC, THIS IS RICKY.

Nothing happened.

Ricky tried again, remembering their emergency code. AAP. But there was no response from the Alec Accounting Program. He waited for a long time but no answering message came on the screen. No question about it. The batteries in the compulator hadn't failed.

Calling to Timcat, Ricky got up and went upstairs. He slipped off his jacket and hung it in the hall closet. Then he went into the kitchen. Timcat ate the piece of leftover chicken Ricky got from the refrigerator for him, then rubbed against his ankles, hoping for a treat from Ricky's snack. But Ricky sat down at the kitchen table without getting anything to eat. He shook his

head at Timcat. "Sorry," he said softly. "I'm not hungry." He stared out the window. How would he solve the gradepoint mystery without ALEC? Why had he disappeared? Was he gone forever?

It was still dark the next morning when Ricky's alarm sounded. He groaned, fumbled in the darkness until he turned off the buzzer, then settled back down on his pillow. He fell asleep, only to wake up again a few minutes later. He had to get up if he was going to pay Dickson Junior High an early morning visit.

He scrambled out of bed and dressed quickly. Downstairs he stopped long enough to feed Timcat and eat a bowl of cereal himself. Then he wrote a note for Mom and Dad, telling them he'd gone out for a walk. He patted Timcat good-by and grabbed his jacket.

The sun was just casting its first light as he left the house, and prickles of rain blew into his face. Still, it was no more than a sprinkle, so he pulled his jacket closer and went on. It would be a long walk to Dickson, but he didn't want to bother with hiding his bike once he got there.

When he finally came within sight of the school, Ricky felt his throat tighten with excitement. He didn't know what he expected to find there, but who could tell what a little exploring might turn up? Someone at Dickson *had* to be behind the gradepoint mystery, and maybe that someone had left clues behind.

Ricky was so busy with his thoughts, he nearly tripped over the railroad tracks that ran parallel to the school grounds. Dickson Junior High was one of the oldest buildings in town. The rambling, red brick structure looked like an ancient fortress in the early morning light, and Ricky suddenly wished he'd asked a friend along. He gave himself a mental shake. He'd already decided against that. If he were caught, there might be trouble; he couldn't ask Karen or Jason to take that risk.

Now that he was actually at the school, it was hard to know where to begin. Cautiously he crept closer, peering through the hedges that edged the front of the building. He found an opening, pushed through, and pressed his face against a window. Only a classroom.

He moved on to the next set of windows, leaning close to look inside. His heart beat faster. There was a terminal in the room, and someone was bending over it. A second person hovered nearby. Both of them had their backs to Ricky, but something about them seemed familiar. He leaned closer, hoping to recognize the pair. . . .

Wham! Something hit him from behind. His only thought was that his head was going to hurt something awful. Then everything went black.

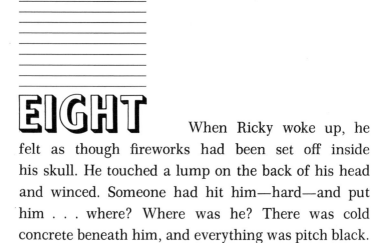

EIGHT

When Ricky woke up, he felt as though fireworks had been set off inside his skull. He touched a lump on the back of his head and winced. Someone had hit him—hard—and put him . . . where? Where was he? There was cold concrete beneath him, and everything was pitch black. He fought his rising fear, trying not to panic.

Slowly he sat up, his head swimming. When the dizziness passed, he got to his feet. Then he carefully stepped forward, reaching out until his hands came into contact with a cold, rough-textured wall. He groped his way along it, trying not to think of the spiders that might have taken refuge in the place— wherever it was.

From the musty smell, Ricky suspected he was in a basement or some other underground room. He stumbled against what seemed to be a piece of wooden furniture, righted himself, then ran his hands over the object. It was an old-fashioned school desk—the kind that were placed in rows so that the front of one desk served as seat for the desk ahead. South Street had newer-style desks, made all in one piece.

As he felt his way along he found more and more desks, dozens of them, each covered with a thick layer of dust. Finally he ran out of desks and came to open space and saw something that made his heart beat faster.

A light. A tiny sliver of light just ahead!

He rushed toward it and found it came from a thin crack around a door. Full of hope, he tried the knob and pushed against the door. It was solid and unyielding. He was locked in.

Panic hit him again. He had to get out! "Help!" he shouted. "I'm locked in here! Get me out!" He kept on yelling until he was hoarse. Then he stopped to listen and give his voice a break.

He could hear rain pattering distantly against the thick door, so apparently it led directly outside. But nothing else stirred.

He began to yell again, but after a moment the noisy roar of a train drowned out his voice, so he had to give up until it passed.

The train seemed particularly long, and there was a great deal of clanging and banging as though cars were being switched. Dejectedly Ricky sank down on the floor, pulling his jacket more closely around him as protection against the damp chill of the place.

His hand touched something hard in the jacket

pocket. Of course! The compulator! Hope glimmered in his brain like the tiny sliver of light around the cellar door. If only he could contact ALEC.

With nervous, fumbling fingers he keyed in the contact code. How long could ALEC stay mad at him? Would he still refuse to answer? Or, worst of all, was he gone forever?

Ricky's heart jumped as the glowing letters began to appear on the face of the compulator: WHERE HAVE YOU BEEN? I WAS GETTING WORRIED.

Under other circumstances it might have seemed funny, but Ricky knew ALEC was trying to say he was sorry for getting angry and refusing to communicate. I AM IN TROUBLE, he typed. The little compulator seemed to be working so slowly!

GIVE ME THE DETAILS. ALEC got straight to business.

SOMEONE HIT ME ON THE HEAD WHILE I WAS EX-PLORING THE DICKSON SCHOOL GROUNDS. WHEN I CAME TO, I WAS LOCKED IN A DARK, UNDERGROUND PLACE.

The answer came slowly. YOU WERE AT DICKSON JUNIOR HIGH?

YES. BUT I COULD HAVE BEEN PUT IN A CAR AND TAKEN SOMEPLACE WHILE I WAS OUT.

The glowing light on the little compulator dimmed, then came on again. Ricky keyed in frantically, ALEC, WHAT'S HAPPENING?

YOUR POWER SOURCE IS DWINDLING.

The batteries were running out. A picture flashed

through Ricky's mind of the new batteries he'd left lying by the microcomputer the night before. But it didn't do any good thinking about that now. The main thing was to give ALEC as much information about this place as he could.

Ricky was suddenly conscious of quiet outside. I HEARD A TRAIN NEARBY, he keyed, trying to choose words sparingly. NOTHING IN CELLAR BUT OLD DESKS. OUTSIDE DOOR LOCKED SOLID.

The light on the compulator flickered again and Ricky swallowed hard. It was going to be awfully lonely in here when he didn't have ALEC to talk to. WHAT HAVE YOU FOUND OUT ABOUT THE GRADEPOINT MYSTERY? he asked, more to keep the communication going than for any other reason.

INFORMATION ON TWO STAFF MEMBERS OF CAS-CADE SCHOOL SYSTEM. THE DICKSON ADVISOR, JONA-THAN SMITH, WAS EMPLOYED AFTER THE SCHOOL YEAR STARTED. HE REPLACED A TEACHER WHO BECAME ILL.

Mr. Smith! Ricky thought. Funny he'd never heard the Dickson's advisor's name before. And it was also the name of the anonymous donor behind the grade-point contest.

The communication from ALEC continued almost frantically, as though he was fearful of running out of time. THE NEW JANITOR AT SOUTH STREET ALSO WORKS AT DICKSON.

MR. ALOYSIUS? Ricky keyed in, surprised.

The light on the compulator died and came on again

only after a long pause. THAT IS THE NAME. BUT IT IS MOST ODD. AS FAR AS THE DATA SHOWS, HE SEEMS TO HAVE NO PAST. NO SOCIAL SECURITY NUMBER—

The light went out and communication stopped abruptly. No matter what Ricky tried, he couldn't bring the compulator to life again. The batteries were dead.

Now that he was cut off from ALEC he felt worse. Sure, ALEC knew what a spot he was in, but how could he figure out where Ricky was? And what could he do about it anyway?

Ricky decided he had to get himself out of this mess. He searched through the room and finally turned up a strong, flat piece of wood that had broken off one of the old desks.

Just what he needed. He wedged the board into the crack at the edge of the door, determined to pry it open, then pushed with all his strength. He felt something give and hope surged through him. But then the board split apart with a loud crack.

Another good idea down the drain!

Once again Ricky sat down. He was cold and dusty. It seemed hours since he'd come to and forever since he'd eaten that cereal. He wished he'd put a piece of fruit or a chocolate bar in his pocket before starting out. But even more than food, he wanted water. His mouth felt desert dry.

To keep his mind off his problems, he reviewed the information ALEC had given him. The fact that Mr.

Aloysius worked at both schools made him a prime suspect. And he did seem to spend a lot of time around the computer room. Abruptly Ricky remembered something. When he'd gone back to school the night before, he'd found Mr. Aloysius sweeping the computer room. But the janitor had already swept there, during the computer club meeting! Was sweeping only his excuse for being near the computer again?

Ricky shook his head. None of it made any sense. What reason could an elderly janitor have for rigging grades?

A sudden sound jarred him from his thoughts. Someone was out there! "Help!" he shouted. "Let me out! I'm locked in here! Help! Help!"

His efforts were rewarded by a loud bark. His "rescuer" was only a stray dog.

He sank down again, feeling totally hopeless. No one would rescue him. He'd die of starvation, and his ghost would haunt Dickson forever. He had a sudden image of Kirk Stevens's face as he met the Ghost of Ricky Foster, and he laughed. "Can't give up," he said out loud. The sound of his own voice helped a little.

He thought he heard a noise again. It was probably only the dog, but he had to try. "Help!" he called, though not as loud as before. "Help, I'm trapped in here!"

He almost fell over when a voice replied. Even though the words were too muffled to be understood, he'd never heard a more welcome sound. He pressed his face close to the door. "I'm locked in," he shouted. "I can't get out."

"Ricky!" He recognized Karen's clear, high voice. "Is that you?"

"It's me," he shouted back. "Get me out."

Someone banged and tugged at the door and he pushed against it, trying to help. But it wouldn't give way.

"We can't get the door open," Karen called to him. "Wait right there while we go for help."

Ricky grinned. "I'll wait," he said. "I'm not going anywhere."

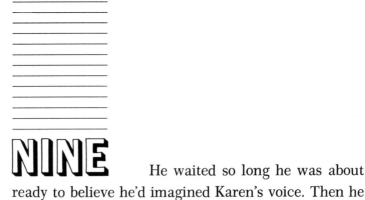

NINE

He waited so long he was about ready to believe he'd imagined Karen's voice. Then he heard the sound of someone fumbling with a lock.

"I'll have it open in a minute." Ricky knew that voice. It was Mr. Smith, the Dickson advisor. Had help come or had his attacker returned?

In a flash Ricky moved deep into the room, crouching down behind one of the old desks. The door swung open, and even though it was a gray, rainy day, the light seemed blinding.

"I don't see anyone," the Dickson advisor said. "This place has been locked up for ages. I don't know why you dragged me out on a wild goose chase."

"We have information that Ricky Foster is here," said a voice that rang with authority.

It was Mr. Aloysius! Ricky didn't move. He didn't know whom to trust.

"We checked with Ricky's parents, and they said

he'd left the house early. They hadn't seen him all morning." That was Jason.

Ricky had already begun to edge his way toward the door when he heard Karen. "I know he's in there. I heard him calling."

"Here I am," Ricky said, stumbling forward into the light.

His friends greeted him with joyous shouts, and Mr. Aloysius patted him on the shoulder. But Mr. Smith regarded him with a frown. "What were you doing in there anyway?" he asked.

Karen put her hands on her hips. "He was having a great time, couldn't you tell?" she said.

Ricky looked back through the door to the blackness beyond. "I'm just glad to get out," he said. He looked around and was surprised to see he was only a few hundred yards from Dickson Junior High. His prison was an old storage shed built into the hillside close to the railroad tracks.

"What happened?" Jason asked. "How did you get locked in there?"

"Yes," said the Dickson advisor. "I believe you owe us some explanations! You're just lucky I was at school this morning and could find the key to this place. You could have been here forever."

Ricky's legs felt a little wobbly. He was thirsty, tired, and hungry. "I could use some water before I start talking," he said.

"We'll go inside and get you a drink," said Mr. Aloysius.

"I'm not sure you should do that," Mr. Smith protested, looking worried. "It is Saturday, and with the principal not here, I feel responsible."

"It'll be all right," Mr. Aloysius said firmly. "This is an emergency."

Ricky glanced at the white-haired man. Mr. Aloysius seemed different, more sure of himself. He spoke as though he were used to being in charge.

When Mr. Aloysius got the door open, Ricky hurried down the darkened corridor. When he found a fountain, he drank eagerly. Cold water never tasted so delicious.

"You sure were thirsty." Karen sounded impressed.

"I left home just about daylight," Ricky explained, then frowned. "What time is it now?"

Jason looked at his watch. "Nearly noon."

"That's later than I guessed. I wonder how long I was out."

"Out?" Mr. Aloysius asked sharply.

"Somebody conked me on the head and threw me in that cellar."

"What!" everyone chorused.

Ricky touched the back of his head with careful fingers. "I have the bump to prove it."

Mr. Aloysius examined Ricky's injured head. "You've got a good-sized bump there, all right."

He wouldn't let anyone ask more questions until

Ricky had had a chance to wash off some of the dust from the storage shed and make himself more comfortable. Then he ushered them all into the deserted school cafeteria and got out some fruit and juice for Ricky.

Mr. Smith watched nervously. "This is strictly against the rules," he said. "You kids shouldn't be here."

Mr. Aloysius ignored the remark. "Why don't you put in a call for a cab to take these young people home," he suggested. "Then let Ricky's parents know that he's safe and sound."

Mr. Smith opened his mouth as if to protest, then thought better of it and stalked away.

Ricky ate the last bite of his apple and drained the juice. "How did you know where to find me?"

Karen and Jason looked at each other. "We were at school early for the computer club meeting," said Karen. "Mr. Aloysius was there, too."

So Mr. Aloysius had been hanging around the computer room again, thought Ricky. He didn't like the way the evidence was stacking up.

"Karen and I were working with the computer when the screen blanked out," continued Jason. "After a second or two, a message appeared. It said, 'Look for Ricky in the old storage shed at Dickson Junior High.'"

Karen picked up the story. "We thought it was a joke until we called your parents and found you'd been gone so long they were beginning to worry."

Mr. Aloysius spoke slowly. "Only thing I can figure

is that whoever tossed you into that place got worried and wanted to let your friends know where to find you."

"It's possible," said Karen, "but how could anyone access the computer to get the message on it?"

"It isn't all that hard to find out an access code," said Jason. "Especially in a system like ours, where so many people use the computer."

Karen and Jason started talking about how someone could have acquired the code, and Ricky let the discussion go on around him without taking part. He had no doubts about who had accessed the school computer and arranged his rescue.

Mr. Aloysius brought the conversation back to Ricky's adventure. "You're sure it wasn't just a nasty joke played on you by someone in the computer club?" he suggested.

"Positive," said Jason. "No one in the club would hit Ricky over the head."

"He's the Microkid," said Karen, as if this explained everything.

"But someone from the Dickson club might do it," Jason said thoughtfully. Ricky knew he was thinking of Kirk Stevens.

"That reminds me, Ricky," said Karen. "What were you doing here anyway?"

At that moment Mr. Smith returned. "I hate to make accusations," he said, "but I'm afraid I know what you were doing here, Ricky Foster. You were falsifying records so Dickson would lose the gradepoint contest."

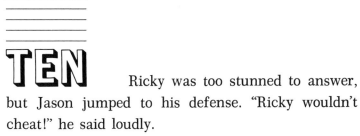

TEN

Ricky was too stunned to answer, but Jason jumped to his defense. "Ricky wouldn't cheat!" he said loudly.

"And he sure didn't knock himself out and throw himself in that shed!" Karen sounded as mad as Jason.

"Good point." Mr. Aloysius looked questioningly at the Dickson advisor. "What makes you think the records have been tampered with?"

"A few days ago, someone lowered the grades by computer. And just now, when I went in to check the records, I found all the grade reports had been erased."

"Just like at South Street!" Karen exclaimed.

Mr. Smith went on. "A hundred thousand dollars is a large sum of money. The temptation must have been too great." He shook his head sadly.

Ricky was so furious his head hurt again, but he tried not to let the anger show when he spoke. "We've had lots of complaints that grades were changed at

South Street," he said, trying to watch the reactions of both men.

"A coverup," Mr. Smith insisted. "Lies to conceal what you were doing to our computer."

"Ask the teachers at our school," Karen insisted.

"Look at my six weeks' report," Jason added. "Two of my grades had to be changed."

The Dickson advisor shook his head sadly. "I'd like to believe you, but let me tell you what I've discovered right here in—"

Mr. Aloysius lifted a restraining hand. "Later. Right now we need to get Ricky home."

Mr. Smith stayed inside while the white-haired man led the way out. He walked slowly, as though he were tired and depressed.

Just outside the door they almost collided with Kirk and his two friends. "What are you boys doing here today?" Mr. Aloysius asked sharply.

Kirk straightened, trying to look tough. "We came back to talk to Mr. Smith again. Anyway, we sure don't have to answer to a janitor." He turned to his friends for support. "What I want to know is, what are those three twerps doing at our school?"

One of the other boys stepped forward. "They're probably here to mess up our computer," he said.

Kirk nodded. "You can't get away with it," he told Ricky. "Our advisor's onto you, and he's a real expert. He knows how to play all kinds of tricks with a computer."

Ricky didn't get a chance to reply. Mr. Aloysius stepped between the two groups, looking stormy. "Go on, boys," he said. He watched as they went on up to the door, where they were admitted by Mr. Smith.

Ricky's mind raced. What did Kirk mean about coming back again? Had the boys been there earlier? Had Kirk and his friends been responsible for his imprisonment?

Mr. Aloysius led the way to the curb, where a cab was waiting. "Ricky, tell your parents I'll be talking to the police about this matter," he said softly. He put a bill into the driver's hand. "These young people will tell you where they live."

Karen, Ricky, and Jason climbed into the back seat. On the way home they talked about what had happened, but nobody came up with any answers. Ricky was dropped off first.

Mom and Dad tried not to make a fuss, but when they heard about the blow to his head, they put him in the car and drove straight to the emergency room. The young doctor there examined him and told him to take it easy for the rest of the weekend and to call if he started feeling dizzy or nauseous.

It seemed to Ricky that everything was getting in the way of his contacting ALEC. When they got back home, he half expected Mom and Dad to object when he said he wanted to go work with the microcomputer, but they didn't. He left them in the living room, still talking about his adventures, and hurried down the

steps. His head hardly hurt any more. Besides, he was well aware that ALEC would be worrying about him.

He set up the phone communication and keyed in the contact code. ALEC, THIS IS RICKY.

RICKY! ARE YOU ALL RIGHT?

I'M FINE. MY FRIENDS AT SCHOOL GOT YOUR MESSAGE AND RESCUED ME. HOW DID YOU DO IT? HOW DID YOU FIGURE OUT WHERE I WAS?

A SIMPLE EXERCISE IN LOGIC. ALEC was offhand. A MATTER OF SCANNING CITY ARCHITECTURAL PLANS. TAKING IN THE FACTOR OF THE STORED DESKS, I STARTED WITH EDUCATIONAL INSTITUTIONS. THE VICINITY OF DICKSON JUNIOR HIGH WAS SUSPECT, OF COURSE, AND THE LOCATION COORDINATED WITH THE SCHEDULED RUN OF TRAINS.

Ricky grinned. A SIMPLE MATTER?

CERTAINLY. I SIMPLY TRANSMITTED THE INFORMATION TO THE SCHOOL COMPUTER, REALIZING THAT YOUR FRIENDS WOULD BE GATHERING FOR THEIR MEETING.

Ricky barely remembered having mentioned the meeting to ALEC. ANYWAY, THANKS FOR FIGURING OUT HOW TO RESCUE ME. NOW I DON'T SUPPOSE YOU'VE FIGURED OUT WHO HIT ME ON THE HEAD AND LOCKED ME IN THE CELLAR?

It was meant to be a joke, but ALEC responded immediately. IT WOULD SEEM THAT YOU WERE STRUCK TO KEEP YOU FROM WITNESSING SOMETHING.

I DON'T KNOW WHAT IT COULD BE. I JUST SAW A

COUPLE OF PEOPLE AT THE COMPUTER. The picture of what he'd seen replayed itself in his mind. THEIR BACKS WERE TO ME, SO I COULDN'T RECOGNIZE THEM.

NOT THE JANITOR?

Ricky shook his head, then realized what he was doing. ALEC couldn't see him. MR. ALOYSIUS IS CHUNKY, BIGGER THAN EITHER OF THOSE GUYS. A sudden thought occurred to him. THEY COULD HAVE BEEN KIDS, BIGGER THAN JASON OR ME, BUT— He broke off, trying to put things together in a way that made sense. WHOEVER WAS IN THAT ROOM DIDN'T HIT ME.

BUT IT IS POSSIBLE THAT YOU WERE STRUCK TO KEEP YOU FROM IDENTIFYING WHOMEVER WAS IN THAT ROOM. I AM PLEASED YOUR INJURIES WERE NOT MORE SERIOUS.

Ricky grinned. WERE YOU WORRIED ABOUT ME, ALEC?

I KEPT MYSELF OCCUPIED, responded ALEC, sidestepping the question. WHILE I WAITED FOR YOUR RESCUE, I SCANNED FOR RELEVANT INFORMATION.

WHAT DID YOU DIG UP?

THE DIRT ON THE NEW JANITOR, replied ALEC.

TELL ME, OR YOUR NAME'S MUD, Ricky typed. Two could play that game.

HE LIVES AT 2400 HILLSIDE DRIVE, responded ALEC, ignoring Ricky's joke. IT'S ON THE NORTH EDGE OF

TOWN, AN UNUSUAL PLACE FOR A JANITOR TO LIVE.

WHY UNUSUAL? asked Ricky.

TAX ASSESSMENT RECORDS SHOW PROPERTY IN THIS AREA TO BE VERY EXPENSIVE. ACCORDING TO MY COMPARATIVE ANALYSIS, MR. ALOYSIUS'S SALARY IS 10% HIGHER THAN THE NATIONAL AVERAGE FOR JANITORS WITH ONE TO THREE YEARS' EXPERIENCE. HOWEVER, THIS SUM WOULD NOT ALLOW HIM TO MAINTAIN A HOME AT 2400 HILLSIDE WITHOUT OUT-SIDE INCOME.

Ricky drew a deep breath. MAYBE HE'S A CARE-TAKER THERE, he suggested. IN ANY CASE, I THINK IT'S TIME I HAD A LONG TALK WITH HIM. I'M GOING OUT THERE NOW.

THIS TIME, REMEMBER THE BATTERIES FOR THE COMPULATOR, scolded ALEC. I DO NOT LIKE BEING CUT OFF IN THE MIDDLE OF A TRANSMISSION.

Ricky laughed, but he replaced the batteries immediately. Then he signed off and went upstairs.

How was he going to get to Hillside Drive? How, in fact, was he going to get out of the house? After what the doctor had said about taking it easy, his parents would be watching him like twin hawks. Well, he'd have to play it by ear.

His parents stopped talking when he came into the living room. "Ricky, your father and I have been discussing what happened to you," said Mom.

"We know there's a strong rivalry between Dickson

and South Street, but knocking you out and locking you up is a criminal act!" Dad shook his head. "We can't ignore it, Ricky."

"Mr. Aloysius said he'd call the police," said Ricky.

Dad nodded. "I spoke to them, too. Apparently Mr. Aloysius didn't mention the competition—or Kirk Stevens."

"I'll admit Kirk is a twerp," said Ricky, deliberately using the name Kirk had called him, "but I don't think he or his friends locked me in that storage shed—or did any of the other stuff."

"What 'other stuff'?" Mom asked, sounding alarmed.

Ricky had no choice but to tell them the whole story about the lowered grades and the erased records.

"But why would someone deliberately tamper with your grades?" asked Dad.

Mom nudged him with her elbow. "Remember the hundred thousand dollars," she said.

"But if Ricky's right and it's not the Dickson students, who could it be?" said Dad. "It's not a cash award. No one could get his hands on the actual money."

"I think Mr. Aloysius might have some answers for us," said Ricky. "Can you drive me to his house?"

"If you feel up to it," said Mom. "I think your father and I would like to get to the bottom of this as soon as possible."

On their way out the door, the Fosters ran into Jason and Karen.

"We wanted to make sure you were okay," said Karen.

"Come on with us," Ricky said, climbing into the back seat of the car. "I think we're going to solve the gradepoint mystery."

Jason and Karen were full of questions, but Ricky forestalled them. "It's no sense asking me anything," he said. "I don't have any answers." Without further explanation, he gave his father the address.

"This is the old Hillside Estate," Dad muttered when they finally reached a gateway marked 2400 and turned up a long drive that led to a towering mansion. "Son, are you sure Mr. Aloysius lives here?"

Ricky didn't answer. He wasn't sure. He could only hope ALEC's information was right—and that no one would ask how he'd gotten the address.

The mansion was imposing enough to make anyone think twice about a casual visit. It was built of gray stone and looked more like a castle than a home.

"We could play Dungeons and Dragons here for real," whispered Jason.

"At least it doesn't have a moat," said Karen.

Dad parked the car, and they all tiptoed over to the huge door, as if they were tresspassing and didn't want to be caught.

When Ricky rang the doorbell, chimes sounded from within. A dignified-looking butler answered the door.

He looked them over. "Are you friends of Mr. Smith?" he inquired.

"Uh, who?" Ricky asked.

The man took on a patient look. "This is the residence of Mr. A. J. Smith," he said.

Suddenly everything was clear to Ricky. "Tell him it's Ricky, Karen, and Jason," he said.

The man looked a little doubtful, but he led them inside. "Please wait here." He pointed to chairs in the huge entrance hall.

A moment later, he came back. "If you are Ricky Foster, Jason Lindsay, and Karen Fujisawa, you may see Mr. Smith now."

"Guess that leaves us out." Martin Foster frowned.

"We'll wait here, Ricky," Mom told him.

Ricky and the others followed the butler into a book-lined room. An elegantly dressed, white-haired man stood in front of a fireplace. It was Mr. Aloysius.

ELEVEN

Ricky walked to the middle of the room. "Mr. Aloysius J. Smith," he said as though making an introduction. "The donor of the hundred-thousand-dollar prize."

Jason and Karen gasped.

Mr. Aloysius smiled slightly. "That was supposed to be a secret," he said. "But I should have known a smart boy like you would figure it out."

"You're giving the prize?" Jason asked. "But janitors don't make that much money!"

Karen looked bewildered. "I've heard of A. J. Smith," she said. "He's a famous inventor. He and his wife are always giving away their money to help young people. Is he you? I mean, are you him?"

"Yes," said Mr. Aloysius, looking uneasy, as though the idea of being famous didn't appeal to him. "Long ago, I was a student at South Street Junior High. I like to think I had the kind of bright, inquiring mind you three have. And now that I have the means, I do what I can to encourage that intellectual curiosity."

"If you went to South Street, why didn't you just give our school the prize?" Jason asked indignantly.

Mr. Aloysius chuckled. "Well, you see, my wife, Eleanor, attended Dickson as a girl. We have a friendly bet going as to which is the better school." The laughter faded from his voice. "Besides, I think the new equipment will be put to best use by the students who feel they've *earned* it."

This was the difficult moment. "You feel that way because of your nephew, don't you?" Ricky asked calmly.

Mr. Aloysius turned abruptly to face the crackling fire. "What do you know about Jonathan?"

Ricky swallowed hard. The last thing he wanted was to hurt Mr. Aloysius. "You told me about him once. You said he was spoiled and didn't think he should have to earn his own way."

Mr. Aloysius turned to face him. "He has a job now."

"But you recommended him for it?"

After a minute Mr. Aloysius nodded. "What are you trying to tell me, Ricky?"

"I think you're already beginning to guess that your nephew rigged the computers to lower the grades at both schools—and then erased the records."

"Why would he do a thing like that?" Mr. Aloysius asked angrily. When Ricky didn't answer, he went over to pick up a phone. "Jonathan, come down to the library right away," he said, then hung up.

When the door opened, they all turned expectantly toward it, but it was the Fosters.

"I insist on knowing what's going on here," Dad said firmly.

"These are my parents," Ricky said to Mr. Aloysius. "They drove us out here."

Before Mr. Aloysius could reply, a tall man strode through the door. "What's the idea of ordering me down here like—" He stopped abruptly at the sight of the small crowd gathered in the library.

Karen and Jason were frozen with shock, but Ricky wasn't surprised to see the Dickson advisor. Mom had been wrong when she'd guessed that the donor's name wasn't Smith, that no one was really named Smith. Actually, there were *two* Mr. Smiths.

"What are these people doing here, Uncle Aloysius?" Mr. Smith asked.

"They have a right to be here, Jon," said Mr. Aloysius. "They're concerned about the falsified grades and the attack on young Ricky here."

"I *told* you the students at both schools were cheating. I *told* you no one deserved the prize," said Mr. Smith, his voice turning shrill. "But you had to play dress-up and go investigate for yourself."

"So that's why you went to work as a janitor," said Jason.

Ricky turned to Mr. Aloysius. "Do you think we cheated?" he asked quietly.

"I found no evidence that the students tampered

with the grades," he said, sinking into a chair, as if he were suddenly worn out. "You did it, didn't you, Jon? You said this time would be different. You'd stick with your career. So I sent you to the computer training program and found you a good job—and this is how you use it: programming a computer to cheat children out of an educational opportunity."

"He may have done the programming at South Street," said Ricky, "but I think he tricked Kirk and the others into doing the dirty work at Dickson." He turned to Mr. Smith. "You fooled them pretty well," he said. "They probably had no idea they were erasing their own grades when they followed your instructions this morning."

Mr. Smith's face was turning an angry red. "Those little creeps," he muttered. "What did they tell you—"

"They didn't tell me anything," Ricky interrupted. "But when we ran into Kirk at school, he let it drop that he'd seen you earlier. That's why you hit me, isn't it? So I wouldn't catch Kirk at the computer and compare notes with him and maybe come up with some interesting conclusions?"

Jonathan Smith looked around, as if he might run for it. But Ricky's dad stood firmly between him and the door.

"It's your own fault," Mr. Smith said sullenly. "You shouldn't have stuck your nose in things, just when I'd set them up so perfectly. Both schools would

accuse each other of cheating and of erasing the grades as a cover-up. And the contest would be such a big mess, Uncle Aloysius would have to cancel it." He stamped his foot. "It's *my* money!" he shouted at his uncle. "I'm your only relative, and I have my rights. You can't keep giving away my fortune. There won't be anything left for me when you die."

A wave of shock and disappointment passed over Mr. Aloysius's face. "It isn't your money, Jon, and now it never will be," he said. "Eleanor and I would never leave such a trust in irresponsible hands." He turned to the Fosters. "I'll go call the police," he said. "Assault—tampering with school records—it can't go unpunished." He got up and left the room, walking as if he'd aged ten years in the last ten minutes.

Mrs. Foster turned on Jonathan Smith. "How long would you have left Ricky in that storage shed?" she demanded.

"I was going to let him out," Mr. Smith said. "I don't know why you're so mad at me. I didn't hit him that hard. . . ." his voice trailed off and his eyes fell before her steely glare. He didn't even put up a struggle when the butler led him away to await the police.

Mr. Aloysius returned, and it was obvious to Ricky that he was making an effort to regain his composure, now that he'd faced the worst.

"What I don't get is how Mr. Smith changed our grades in the first place," said Jason.

"Yeah," said Karen. "He must have sneaked into

South Street at least twice, but the school is usually locked up tight. So how did he get in?"

Mr. Aloysius smiled ruefully. "I'm afraid I know the answer to that one," he said.

"The rock!" said Ricky, suddenly remembering.

"That's right," said Mr. Aloysius. "I propped the back door open with a rock on the nights I had to work late. That way Jonathan could get in when he came by to help me finish up." He sighed. "Now I realize he only offered to help so he'd have access to the computer."

"He probably sneaked in early," offered Karen. "Then, when he'd finished reprogramming the computer, he pretended to be just arriving."

"I'm going to hate telling Eleanor about Jon," said Mr. Aloysius, "though we've been afraid all along . . . ." He broke off as if he didn't want to talk about his nephew any more. "But she'll feel better when she meets you fine young people." He beamed approval at Ricky, Jason, and Karen.

"They've done a great job," said Dad.

"We can be proud of them," agreed Mom.

"But we didn't do anything," said Jason, sounding dazed. "It was Ricky who figured everything out."

"I always knew you were good with computers," said Karen, "but I didn't know you were a good detective, too."

"Maybe we should call you Sherlock Holmes instead of the Microkid," suggested Jason.

Mr. Aloysius chuckled. "That sharp mind should come in handy when we get the contest underway again. I'm going to tell Eleanor that her school doesn't stand a chance with Ricky Foster on the other side."

Ricky felt uncomfortable with so much praise. At least half the credit should have gone to ALEC, but there was no way he could tell his friends that. He'd just have to pass on ALEC's share of the compliments when he got back home to the microcomputer.

"Come on, Ricky, tell us how you cracked the case," insisted Jason.

"Uh, just logic and a little luck," he said. And a lot of ALEC, he added mentally.